Hairline Cracks

ugitives have to sleep somewhere. Luckily it was
mmer. I went upstairs and burrowed under my bed.
ollected a lot of dust before I found my sleeping bag.
was with a plastic poncho which can be used as a
oundsheet.

I pulled open a few drawers at random, looking for
her things a fugitive might need. I decided against the
mpass but took the imitation Swiss Army penknife
d gave me last birthday. On my bedside table was
mall torch; I chucked that in the rucksack as well.

Mo appeared in the doorway of my room. She had
isc in one hand.

"Do you think I could borrow this? It's a new word
ocessing program. I've not seen it before."

I shrugged. "All right." I had other things on my
nd. Mum wasn't in any position to object to the loan.

Suddenly we both became very still. We'd heard the
me sound. It came from the hall.

It was the sound of a key turning in the lock of the
ont door.

Titles by Andrew Taylor available in Lions

Hairline Cracks
Snapshot
Double Exposure
Negative Image

HAIRLINE CRACKS

Andrew Taylor

Lions
An Imprint of HarperCollins*Publishers*

First published in the U.K. in 1988 in Armada
This Lions edition first published in 1992

Lions is an imprint of
HarperCollins Children's Books, a division of
HarperCollins Publishers Ltd,
77–85 Fulham Palace Road,
Hammersmith, London W6 8JB

Printed and bound in Great Britain by
HarperCollins Manufacturing, Glasgow

CHAPTER ONE

Friday was a bad day right from the start.

Just before I got home I remember thinking that at least it couldn't get worse. I was wrong.

I'd been over to Mo's flat that afternoon but all I found was a message for me on the door. "Gone to the seaside," she'd written. "My parents think they're doing me a favour. See you tomorrow." So I'd walked a mile and a half for nothing.

The afternoon carried on downhill all the way. The weather was hot and sticky. I hung around the shopping centre for a bit, mostly in the new games arcade next to Woolworth's. Shopping centres and games arcades aren't much fun when you haven't any money.

Roland and his gang came into the arcade. They're in the class above ours at school and like to think they're a sort of junior Mafia. Roland's been gunning for me and Mo since we turned down his kind offer to protect us from him for a mere fifty pence a week.

Things turned nasty as they usually do when Roland's around.

"Sam Lydney," he sneered with his fake American accent. "Just the guy I want to see."

I swerved to avoid his fist and ran into the street. The whole pack of them came tumbling after me. I started running. They're all bigger than me and on a level track they would have caught me in seconds. But this was a crowded shopping precinct and anyway all of them smoke too much.

I lost them in the big department store by the sunken roundabout. After that, there was no point in staying around. I headed for home, walking quickly and glancing back to make sure they weren't behind me.

We live in a long, grimy street just beyond the railway station. There are terraced houses on both sides of the road. Some of them have been knocked down, so the street looks like an open mouth with some of its teeth missing.

I could tell our house was empty as soon as I opened the front door. Normally that wouldn't have surprised me because my mum doesn't get back from work until after six, and it was only four o'clock. But she was having a day off and she hadn't said she was going out.

Usually she leaves messages on the notice board in the kitchen. I checked but there was nothing there – just the bills and shopping lists.

There was a casserole in the oven which reminded me that Davis was coming for supper tonight. I don't know why he and my mum don't get married. He spends more time with us than he does at his flat.

I poured myself some orange juice, dropped in a couple of ice cubes and sat down at the table. I noticed the washing-up from lunch hadn't been done. Mum had offered to do it for me today because I was in a hurry to get to Mo's. It was odd she hadn't bothered – she's fanatical about washing-up. I think it shows she's mentally unbalanced.

Then I saw her coffee mug. It was on the floor by one of the table legs. I picked it up and found there was a small puddle of coffee under the table. If the unwashed plates were odd, the coffee cup and the puddle on the floor were downright weird.

That's how it all began: unwashed plates and a coffee cup on the floor. At the time I thought she must have had to go out in a hurry. Maybe she was meeting Davis and was late. Maybe Mrs Jones next door had had another nervous breakdown.

I got up and wandered through the house. I suppose I was looking for clues but I didn't think of it that way. All the rooms looked just as they had when I last saw them. Mum's bag wasn't in the sitting room. So she must have gone out. or some reason I was restless. I tried watching television but there was nothing worth seeing on any channel. I

6

played the maze game on the computer for about five minutes. That got boring because I knew it so well. I put on some music. Then I turned it off in case the phone rang.

Don't get me wrong – I wasn't panicking or anywhere near it. I just felt vaguely uneasy. It was the sort of feeling you have when you're going to be sick in about ten minutes time though you don't yet know you're going to be sick.

At five o'clock I phoned Davis. I didn't want to sound worried so I thought I'd just ask what time he was coming round this evening. And I'd mention casually that my mother wasn't here.

The phone rang on and on. I imagined Davis sitting at his typewriter trying to write an article: he'd hear the phone and swear; then he'd get up to answer it and trip over something on the way. He's got this tiny attic flat on the top floor of an old house near the university. It's so full of newspapers and other junk that I've never even seen the carpet.

I counted the rings. If Davis wasn't there, his answering machine would take the call. "Hello," his voice would say, "this is Donald Davis." He always talks to the answering machine as if it was an unexploded bomb. "Unfortunately I have been called away. Please leave a message after the bleep and I will call you back as soon as I can."

After twenty rings I gave up. No Davis and no answering machine: that was another odd thing. He's a freelance journalist, you see, and he always connects up the answering machine if he's going out.

Then I wondered if my mother could have gone into the office after all. She works for the council as personal assistant to Giles Viney, the chief planning officer. It would be just like him to invent a crisis on my mother's day off.

I rang the number and asked for my mother's extension. Viney himself answered.

"Hello, Mr Viney. This is Sam Lydney. Is my mother there?"

"No, of course she isn't." He sounded flustered but that was nothing out of the ordinary. "Don't you know she's having a day off?"

"Yes, I do. But –"

"I haven't got time to talk to you," he snapped. "Some people have work to do."

He put the phone down. I blew a raspberry down the line. I don't know how my mother can bear to work for a man like that. I've only met him once. I've never seen a human being who looks so much like a toad.

Doing anything was better than doing nothing. It wasn't likely that my mother had left a message with the neighbours – if she had had that much time she would have written a note for me. But it was worth trying.

I went to the Singhs' first. Mrs Singh opened the door. She was carrying the baby and the hall behind her was a seething mass of children. I've never been quite sure how many little Singhlets there are. The smell of cooking drifted down from the kitchen. My mouth watered.

Mrs Singh hadn't seen my mother since this morning when they met at the corner shop. Nor had any of her children. But I was welcome to have tea with them.

I turned down the offer and tried Mrs Jones. She's a widow and she's lived in the same house for donkey's years. She's OK when she's not having a nervous breakdown, except she suffers from the curious belief that anyone under the age of eighteen adores jelly babies. I ask you.

Mrs Jones was normal enough today but she hadn't seen Mum.

"You can come and wait with me, Sam," she said. "It's not right, letting kids come home to an empty house. Say what you like, a woman's place is in the home."

"I'm not a kid," I said wearily. Even on the doorstep, the smell of cats was overpowering. "Thank you all the same but I think I'll stay at home."

"Please yourself." She began to close the door. Suddenly she stopped and cackled. "Perhaps your mother went off in that big car."

"What big car?"

"Don't often see cars like that round here. Not nowadays, anyway. It was a big white one. It was parked outside."

I questioned her but it wasn't much use. All she knew was that a big white car had been parked outside her house and ours, sometime during the afternoon. She had no idea of the make and she hadn't seen who was in it. What she really wanted to do was tell me how much our street had changed for the worse since she and Mr Jones moved in forty years before. She made it sound as though every house used to have its own Rolls-Royce.

I managed to escape after five minutes. Davis always gets stuck with her for at least half an hour: he says that since meeting Mrs Jones he knows how rabbits feel when they meet a stoat.

Our house felt emptier than ever. I was starving so I made myself a peanut butter sandwich to bridge the gap between now and supper. I made it just the way I like it, which means more peanut butter than bread.

As I ate, I wondered what to do. Suppose Mum had had an accident? Perhaps I should phone the police or the hospital. But I didn't want to do that. They'd think I was scared of being alone in the house or something. Anyway, I had no reason to think that something was wrong. Not then.

And if I told the police, they'd want to get in touch with my father. I didn't want that and I was pretty sure he wouldn't either. I see him every other Saturday and believe me that's quite enough. The police would probably tell him to come and fetch me. I'd have to spend the night at his flat with my stepmother and the baby. Anything was better than that.

I licked the peanut butter off my fingers and tried to phone Davis again. He still wasn't in. I wished I could ring Mo but her parents don't have a telephone. I wondered about leaving a note for my mother and going round to the Singhs'. But I didn't want to leave the house in case she tried to phone me.

In the end the best thing to do was to have another sandwich. Being hungry wouldn't help anyone, least of all me.

By the time I'd finished the second sandwich and scraped out the jar, I'd decided to ring the hospital. I'd lower my voice so I sounded like an adult, and ask if they had a patient called Sue Lydney. I'd say she was my sister.

I didn't really think she'd be in hospital. Someone would have rung up by now – her driving licence and other papers were always in her bag. But it would be nice to know for sure.

I looked up the number and began to dial. Then the door-bell rang. I slammed down the phone and ran into the hall.

My father was standing on the doorstep. It was still hot but he was wearing a jacket and tie. His black BMW was parked behind him with the engine running.

"Hi, Sam." He punched me lightly on the arm as if he was my best mate. "How you doing?"

"Fine," I said. I could see the sweat on his forehead.

"Your mother's had to go away," he said. "You're coming to stay with us for a while."

"Has he wiped his feet?" Maxine said.

They were the first words she said when we got to the flat. And she said them to my father. She doesn't like talking to me directly.

My father nodded.

Maxine glanced at me. Her eyes are so small and pale you hardly notice them, but you could make an inch-thick paintbrush out of her eyelashes. I bet they're false. She was my father's secretary before they got married.

"Will he eat with us?" she said.

"Of course he will." My father tried to ruffle my hair but I managed to get out of reach. "Growing lad – needs all the nourishment he can get."

Maxine left the living room. I could hear her in the kitchen, rattling the saucepans as if she hated them. My father gave me a can of Coke and poured himself a huge whisky. He slumped on the sofa in front of the television. I could see the top of his head: for the first time I realized he was beginning to go bald.

I sat down at the other end of the sofa. They were showing the local news on the TV. My father leant forward to watch. I wondered if he was using it as an excuse not to talk to me. He'd hardly said a word in the car.

The Coke was ice-cold, just the way I like it. But I didn't enjoy it. Dad's flat is the sort of place where you feel you have to be on your best behaviour. It's on the first floor of an old house with pillars round the front door. The living room is so big you could practically fit our house inside it, roof and all. It's got a marble fireplace and two huge windows. The chairs and sofa are covered with slippery black leather.

As I sipped the Coke, I kept one eye on the TV and the other on Dad. The police had rounded up a gang of drug-pushers. A civil servant claimed that the nuclear power station on the estuary was perfectly safe. Someone else said the power station should be closed down because radiation leaks might make it a health hazard. A third person waffled on about the new town they wanted to build nearby. The next item was about a businessman who'd won our local yacht race, the Kingdom Cup. The Mayor presented him with the cup in a ceremony at the old docks. It was all pretty boring and I don't think my father was any more interested than I was. When the adverts came on, I seized my chance.

"Dad, what's happened to Mum?"

He turned to look at me. A roll of fat bulged over the waistband of his trousers. He took a swallow of his drink. It was almost as if he needed it to give him courage. But why did it take courage to talk to me?

"She needed a break, Sam. Working too hard, getting uptight – you know."

"She seemed OK at lunchtime," I said. "And why didn't she say anything to me?"

"Your mother didn't want you to worry. We talked it over together and decided it'd be better this way."

"What way?"

My father waved his glass. "Not telling you until she'd gone. Between ourselves, old son, she couldn't face it. You know how highly strung she is." He winked at me. "Most women are."

If there's one thing I hate, it's my father calling me "old son". And I couldn't help thinking he was talking rubbish. When he and my mum were still living together, he was always the one who lost his temper and started shouting. If that's not being highly strung, I don't know what is. Anyway, Davis says Mum's got nerves of granite. He should know.

I didn't want to start an argument. So all I said was: "How long will she be away?"

Dad shrugged. "A few weeks, maybe longer. It's a sort of

extended holiday."

"But what's going to happen to me?"

"You'll stay with us, of course. That's part of the plan." He gave me another man-to-man wink. "Give you a chance to get to know Henrietta."

I said nothing. Henrietta is my half-sister. She's six months old and easily the most boring person I know. Maxine and my father think she's marvellous.

Dad was still talking. The words came out fast, as if he was trying to sell me something. Perhaps that's only to be expected because he works in advertising. He was saying how pleased they were to have me to stay for longer than a weekend and how we could do all sorts of things together. Maxine was looking forward to getting to know me better. My birthday was coming up in September and they were planning to get me a new bike and maybe some clothes as well.

"Has Mum gone away with Davis?"

My father dried up in mid-sentence. Mentioning Davis often has that effect on him. For the first time this evening he seemed at a loss.

"You know," I said. "Davis."

"I'm not sure," he said slowly. "She didn't say."

The doorbell rang. Dad got up, straightening his tie. He closed the door behind him. I could hear the murmur of voices in the hall.

I stood up too, and wandered across to one of the windows. It seemed to me that they were all in a conspiracy against me – Dad, Maxine, Mum and probably Davis as well. All of them must have known that Mum was going and none of them told me. Why? I wasn't a kid any more.

Another idea was in the back of my mind: suppose Dad was lying? But that didn't make sense. Nothing made sense. I wished I could talk to Mo.

It was still light outside. Dad's house is on top of a hill near the cathedral. The city sprawled away to the horizon. I wondered if my mother was somewhere down there in one of the houses or walking in one of the streets.

I craned out of the window. A white Bentley was parked outside. You see a lot of cars like that in this part of town. As I watched, a man came out of the house. I was directly above him. All I could see was a dark coat and red-gold hair that glinted in the evening sun.

I was back on the sofa by the time my father came into the room.

"While I remember," he said, "could you let me have your key? I promised your mother I'd keep an eye on the house while she's away."

He turned away to pour himself another drink. I keep the latchkey on a piece of string round my neck. It seemed a little strange that my mother hadn't given him a key. But parents often do strange things. I lifted the key over my head and passed it to him.

"What happens if I want to get some more of my stuff?"

"Oh, I'll run you over in the car." Dad looked at his watch which made me feel I was wasting his time. "If you want I'll have a copy made."

It all sounded so reasonable.

"Dinner's ready." Maxine was standing in the doorway, looking at my father.

"Great!" My father rubbed his hands together. "I could eat a horse."

I wondered what he'd do if he found a roast horse waiting for him in the kitchen. Probably he'd say "Great" and hack it up with the electric carving knife.

Henrietta began to cry in her room down the hall. Maxine said, "That's all I need" and went to see what was the matter. Looking sheepish, Dad sidled past me and went after her.

There was a phone on the table by the window. On impulse I picked it up and dialled a number. I counted the rings up to twenty-five.

No Davis. No answering machine.

That night I went to bed early.

I couldn't face sitting on the sofa in front of the telly while

14

my dad drank brandy and Maxine talked about Henrietta. I think they were relieved to see me go.

Their flat has three bedrooms: a big one, which Dad shares with Maxine; a middle-sized one which is Henrietta's; and a tiny guest room. I suppose a guest is just what I am.

I lay in bed with the light out but I didn't sleep. There was too much thinking to do. I couldn't understand how Mum could go off without a word to me. The way Dad told it, it hadn't been a spur-of-the-moment decision. I thought about the casserole she'd left in the oven. Why cook a meal if you know that no one's going to eat it?

After a while my mind started going round in circles. Henrietta wailed and Maxine came to feed her. Then I heard her and my father having an argument in the bathroom.

It's an old house but it's surprising how sound carries. It depends which room you're in. When the house was converted into flats, they changed the layout of the rooms. The living room and the kitchen have got quite thick walls, because they were rooms before in the original house. But the bedrooms and the bathroom are new and they've only got thin partitions between them.

Still talking, Maxine and Dad went into their bedroom. I slid out of bed and tiptoed across the carpet. I put my ear right on the wall.

OK, I was eavesdropping. Davis says the end never justifies the means, but perhaps he's never been as desperate as I was. I had to find out what was happening.

"It's a definite offer then?" Maxine was saying.

"Yes. But he's happy at the comprehensive – "

"I'm not having him here day in, day out. We just haven't the space."

My father moved away and I couldn't hear his reply. But Maxine came over loud and clear:

"It's for his own good, Mark! He needs a bit of discipline, you know that. And think of all the facilities a good boarding school has. He'll thank you for it when he's older. And

15

it's not as if we'd have to pay a penny. It's too good an offer to refuse."

Dad mumbled something.

"Exactly," Maxine said angrily. "We need a much bigger house. And surely he'll help with that? After all, you – "

"Sssh!" said my father.

Henrietta started to howl.

"Poor little love," Maxine cooed. "It's her toothy-pegs. Will you go?"

Sometimes adults make me sick.

I didn't get much sleep that night.

Dad and Maxine were going to send me to some snotty boarding school: that changed everything. It meant that Mum was going to be away for much more than a few weeks. My father had lied to me. I wished I could hate him, the way I hate Maxine. But things weren't that simple.

I didn't want to go to boarding school. I wouldn't see Mo or any of my friends. What was wrong with the Alderman Jessop Comprehensive? Well, lots of things were wrong like Roland and the muck they give us for dinner. But boarding school would be far worse.

I wondered who had offered to pay the fees. And why. There were too many questions and not enough answers to go round. I lay there in the darkness, listening to a church clock striking the quarters and wishing I was home.

Sometime after three o'clock I must have dozed off. The next thing I knew, it was daylight. For a moment I thought yesterday had been a bad dream, the kind you get when you've got a fever. Then I saw where I was.

But the sleep had helped. My mind was clearer and I knew what I was going to do.

I swung my feet out of bed. I hadn't drawn the curtains. The city below had a clean, deserted look. My watch said it was just on six thirty.

My clothes were lying on the floor. I pulled them on as quietly as possible. My suitcase was open: I took out my heavy jacket. If only I had some money.

Carrying my shoes, I tiptoed down the hall. The other bedroom doors were open. Dad was snoring just like he used to do when he still lived with us.

The real problem was the flat's front door. There were two bolts, two locks and a security chain. I forced myself not to hurry. One of the locks screeched. The chain clanked against the door jamb. Each noise nearly gave me a heart attack.

One more bolt and I'd be free.

Henrietta snuffled, coughed and began to wail.

I froze.

Maxine stirred.

Henrietta stopped crying. I could have kissed her. A couple of minutes later I was outside in the street.

I walked fast. It was ten to seven by the time I passed the university tower. I turned into the tree-lined road where Davis lives. That's when things started to go wrong.

A police car was outside the house. On the front doorstep a uniformed sergeant was talking with a man in plain clothes. Another man had emptied out the dustbins in the concrete yard at the front. He was picking through the rubbish with a stick. A huge Alsatian sat beside him.

Davis's car wasn't there. You can't miss it: it's a yellow Deux Chevaux held together by rust and by stickers saying things like "Nuclear Power – No Thanks". Usually he parks it by the dustbins, alongside the students' bikes.

It took me about a second to take all this in. My heart started to thud inside my chest. I slowed down and sauntered along the pavement. The Alsatian looked at me and yawned, showing all its teeth.

For one crazy moment I thought the police were looking for me – that Dad had found I'd left, guessed where I was going and phoned the cops. That was stupid, of course, but it did make me cautious.

I didn't know what to do. The cops would question me if I tried to go into the house. Anyway, it looked as though Davis hadn't come back. And what were the police doing here?

I moved closer, whistling casually under my breath. I don't know who I was trying to fool – myself, maybe. The front door opened and Gary came out. He's one of the students who live there. Apart from Davis's attic flat, the whole house is divided up into bedsits.

Gary always dresses in black to match his skin. He sneered at the sergeant and the sergeant sneered back. Gary's about six feet five so his sneer carried more weight.

He turned left along the road. We were moving in the same direction but he was about fifteen yards in front. The road curves here. In a couple of minutes we were both out of sight of the police.

I ran after him and touched his arm. He swung round as if I'd stung him.

"Gary," I said quickly. "It's me, Sam."

He relaxed and smiled. "How're you doing, Sam?"

We'd met once or twice up in Davis's flat. He's studying law and sometimes he advises Davis on legal points for his stories. He's one of Davis's best friends.

"What's happening back there?" I asked. "And where's Davis?"

The smile vanished.

"You haven't heard?" Gary walked on; I had to run to keep up with him. "The fuzz raided his flat last night," he said over his shoulder. "The Drug Squad. They didn't find Davis but they found half a kilo of heroin."

First Mum, now Davis. Only Mo was left. With my luck I'd probably find she'd gone too. Kidnapped by a white slaver or something.

Still, unless I trailed back to Dad's flat, Mo was the only option I had left. Even Gary didn't want to know me at present. Perhaps he thought I was a drug dealer too.

Mo lives in a tower block of council flats. They've got a great view if you like looking at motorways. Her place is miles away from Davis's flat. By the time I got there I had a blister. I was also on the verge of starvation.

I couldn't go up to the flat because it was too early. Mo's dad would still be at home. He works for the council parks department and usually leaves about eight thirty.

It's not that I minded meeting him. The trouble is, he's always quarrelling with Mo's mum and if you see them together you get caught in the crossfire. I don't know how Mo stands it. I think they ought to get divorced but Mo says they can't because they're Catholic. Anyway, she reckons they quite enjoy yelling at one another. But it's tough luck on her. She's going to leave home as soon as she can, like her brothers and sisters did.

I hung around on the patch of wasteland in front of the block, keeping an eye open for Roland who lives in one of the flats. Mr Connors came out after about five minutes. He was chewing a piece of toast. My stomach rumbled enviously.

He climbed into their old Cortina and drove off towards the motorway. I took the lift to the seventh floor.

Mrs Connors opened the door. Her face fell when she saw it was me.

"I thought it was the postman," she said. "It's a bit early for social calls, isn't it?" She jerked her head towards the

19

kitchen. "Maureen's having her breakfast."

Mo's parents always call her Maureen. She hates it.

The telly was on at full blast in the lounge. Mrs Connors wandered back to it, the heels of her slippers flopping behind her. On the screen two women were doing keep-fit exercises to music. Mrs Connors sank down on the sofa and reached for a cigarette.

Mo was sitting at the kitchen table, shovelling cornflakes into her mouth. I suppose I should try to describe her. She's a month or two older than me and a couple of inches taller. She's got red hair, a lot of freckles and a foul temper. To say I was glad to see her is like saying it sometimes rains in England.

"You're early," she said.

I sat down suddenly. "My mum's disappeared."

"I wish my mum would disappear." She looked sharply at me and pushed the cornflakes across the table. "You'd better have some breakfast."

Between mouthfuls I told her what had happened.

You can't imagine what a relief it was, just being able to tell someone. I gave her all the details I could remember – from the white car that Mrs Jones had seen outside our house to the way that Gary had hurried away from me.

Mo's a good listener, the sort who asks the right questions. By the time I'd finished she knew as much as I did, which was slightly more than nothing.

"OK, let's get this straight," she said. "Your mum had a day off work. Davis was coming round to supper. You went out in the afternoon and she just vanished. Your dad turns up and whisks you off. Says your mum's gone away for a few weeks. Then you find out it's probably going to be much longer than that, and someone's offered to pay for you to go away to school. You try to see Davis and discover the police are after him."

"It can't be true," I interrupted. "That stuff about the drugs, I mean. He's fanatical about drug-pushers. He's always going on about them."

"So where does that leave us?" Mo said. "You saying someone framed him?"

I hadn't thought of it like that before but it was the only explanation, unless I was wrong about Davis. I've known him for years. He's mad, of course – he's got more ideals and causes than I've had hot dinners. But he doesn't care about money and he hates drugs. He had a kid brother, who overdosed himself on heroin.

Mo pulled her ear lobe, a sure sign that she's thinking. "And your mum's probably been kidnapped. And your dad's helping the kidnappers."

That was going too fast for me. "We can't be sure."

"You got a better idea?" Mo shrugged. "I tell you something else: it's no good you going to the police. It'd be your word against your dad's and Maxine's". She laughed without amusement. "Who'd believe you against two adults?"

There was a moment's silence as we let that thought sink in. I was on the edge of panic: I had this horrible feeling that I was caught in a trap. And the trap was closing in on me.

"I'm not going back to Dad's," I said in a small, tight voice.

"You going to run away to sea?"

We both laughed. It wasn't much of a joke. But sometimes you have to laugh if you don't want to burst into tears.

Mo was the first to stop. "It could be worse," she said. "We've got maybe three things on our side."

I was grateful for that "we".

She tugged her ear again and frowned. "We know that someone with a white Bentley may be involved. We know that your dad wanted the key to your house."

"That's two," I said. "What's the third?"

"Whoever's behind this won't be expecting trouble. Not from us. We're just kids, remember? That's what they'll be thinking. And kids don't count."

Forty-five minutes later I was asking Mrs Singh for the spare key.

We had to move fast. Mo thought that Dad might want to

search the house.

There was another reason to hurry: by now he must have realized I'd done a bunk. I was banking on the hope that he'd think I was coming back, so he wouldn't bother to look for me yet. And it was possible that he wouldn't think of looking for me here. The Singhs had moved into our road after Dad moved out. It was unlikely he knew that Mum had given them a key and that they kept an eye on the house when we weren't here.

I could tell Mrs Singh suspected something. She kept asking where my mum was and where I'd spent the night. I said Mum was away and I was staying with Dad; I told her I'd lost my latchkey. I don't think she believed me but there wasn't a lot she could do about it.

I unlocked the front door. A wave of warm, stale air washed over us as Mo and I went into the hall. There were a few letters on the mat. Automatically I picked them up and put them on the table. The house seemed different already. It no longer felt like home. We looked at one another.

"It's like looking for a needle in a haystack," Mo said.

"It's worse than that," I said. "We don't know what the needle looks like. Or even if there is a needle."

"You're a great help." Mo led the way into the kitchen. "You need money, right? Is there any in the house?"

"I could take the housekeeping, I suppose, but – "

"Well, why not?" she said. "No one else is going to use it."

She had a point. Mum keeps the housekeeping money on the kitchen windowsill, in an old tobacco tin which used to belong to Davis. I opened the tin and found two ten pound notes, a five, several pound coins and some loose change. Mum must have been to the bank recently.

"If she knew she was going away," Mo said, "she wouldn't have left all that money lying around. Go on, take it."

It felt like stealing, which was stupid. The money might help me to find Mum. I stuffed it in the pocket of my jeans.

"We'll search the whole house," Mo said briskly. "We're looking for anything unusual."

She really got my goat. Perhaps I was feeling guilty about the money or perhaps taking it confirmed how serious the situation was. Whatever the reason, I flared up, asking her why she always had to be so bossy. After all, it was my mum who was missing and my house we were in.

She flared back. Suddenly we were in the middle of a full-blown quarrel. Mo's face tried to match the colour of her hair. She said she was only trying to help and if she wasn't wanted I had only to say so.

Things were looking ugly when Mrs Jones rapped on the wall that separates our kitchen from hers. She claims that loud noises upset her cats.

Mo mouthed "miaow" at the wall. We both laughed.

"We're wasting time," I said in my normal voice.

"You're right," Mo said, which was her way of saying sorry. "Shall we start with downstairs?"

It didn't take long. We looked round the kitchen, the sitting room and the so-called dining room that's used as a spare bedroom. Mo picked up the mail on the hall table and leafed through it. Most of it looked like bills or circulars but there was one postcard. The picture side was divided into four: a pier, a big hotel, a children's playground in a park, and some rocky but stunted cliffs. In the middle it said: GREETINGS FROM EASTON-ON-SEA.

"That's where we went yesterday," Mo said. "Yuk."

She flipped it over and a jolt like an electric shock went through me.

"It's from Davis," I yelled.

I grabbed it from her. The card was addressed to Mum in Davis's scrawl. No wonder he needs a typewriter. It takes years of training to read his handwriting.

"What's it say?"

" 'Weather lovely,' " I read out. " 'Sea quite warm for the time of year. Having a wonderful time. Wish you were here. Love, Auntie Mabel.' "

Mo looked blankly at me. "But you haven't got an

Auntie Mabel."

"Course I haven't," I snapped. "Davis wrote it."

"Is there anything else? What about the postmark?"

I checked. It was postmarked yesterday from Easton. Apart from the address and the message, there was nothing else on the card except a few dots and scribbles at the bottom where the photo captions were: it looked as though Davis had been trying to get his biro to work.

"It must mean something," I said.

"Maybe it's some sort of code," Mo suggested. "We'd better take it."

We went upstairs. Mum's toothbrush was still in the bathroom. We tried her bedroom next. As far as I could see, she hadn't taken any clothes apart from the ones she was wearing. The empty suitcases were still on top of the wardrobe. My bedroom was exactly how I'd left it.

Mo shrugged. "Well, we tried. At least we got the postcard and the money."

I turned away so she couldn't see my face. I'd hoped to find so much – a clue to the mystery, an explanation for Mum's disappearance, even the reason for the drugs in Davis's flat.

Mo looked at her watch. "Is there anything else you want to get while we're here?"

I nodded. "I might as well. Give me five or ten minutes?"

"OK. Mind if I have a go on the computer?"

"Feel free," I said.

Mo's mad about computers. Mum says Mo knows more about them than she does. I can't see the attraction myself, though some of the games are quite good. I left Mo in Mum's room, leafing through a pile of floppy discs.

I got my rucksack and started in the kitchen. I was trying to be very cool about this. I was going to be a fugitive, right? Dad and the police would be after me. Fugitives need food. I found some biscuits, a packet of cereal and a few apples. Everything else seemed to need cooking in some way. People on the run don't have fully-equipped kitchens at their disposal.

Fugitives have to sleep somewhere. Luckily it was summer. I went upstairs and burrowed under my bed. I collected a lot of dust before I found my sleeping bag. It was with a plastic poncho which can be used as a groundsheet.

I pulled open a few drawers at random, looking for other things a fugitive might need. I decided against the compass but took the imitation Swiss Army penknife Dad gave me last birthday. On my bedside table was a small torch; I chucked that in the rucksack as well.

Mo appeared in the doorway of my room. She had a disc in one hand.

"Do you think I could borrow this? It's a new word processing program. I've not seen it before."

I shrugged. "All right." I had other things on my mind. Mum wasn't in any position to object to the loan.

Suddenly we both became very still. We'd heard the same sound. It came from the hall.

It was the sound of a key turning in the lock of the front door.

CHAPTER FOUR

Have you ever been frightened?

I don't mean worried or gloomy or unhappy or nervous. I'd been all of those things in the last sixteen hours. What I hadn't been was terrified. Believe me, there's a big difference.

Two people were downstairs. I could tell it wasn't Mum or Davis or even Dad by the way they moved. This was a strange house for them.

Mo and I stared at one another for an instant. It was one of those instants which last for ever, like a nightmare does when you're in the middle of it. It's funny what goes through your mind at times like that. Mo has green eyes; but I'd never noticed before that there were flecks of brown scattered over the green like spots on a leopard. Except leopards aren't green. You know what I mean.

"Take a look upstairs, Pete."

The voice was what Davis calls deep purple – posh and carrying like the ones that hammy old actors have. It made my skin crawl.

I grabbed Mo's wrist and pulled her towards the open door of the bathroom. This was my home and we had every right to be here. But at present I couldn't risk being caught. And I didn't trust that voice.

"But what are we looking for, Mr Trubshaw?" The second voice had a whine in it. The sort of whine that reminds you of an electric drill.

Trubshaw sighed. "Papers, of course. Anything with the words Magnox or Histon on it. Or the name of the firm. Is that simple enough for you?"

"Hairy said we had to stick together."

Trubshaw clicked his tongue against his teeth. "I wish

26

you wouldn't refer to him as Hairy. It's so vulgar."

By this time we were in the bathroom. I'd acted on impulse – it's the only room with a bolt on the door. Then I remembered the window.

"But you know what to look for," Pete said. "You've got education."

"Oh, I see. A little reading problem, is it?" Trubshaw sniffed. "Very well. I wonder why you bothered to come."

While he was speaking I was closing the door, inch by inch. I'd forgotten one thing. The hinges needed oiling. They creaked.

"What was that?" Trubshaw said.

Simultaneously Pete said, "Someone's up there."

I shut the door with a bang and rammed home the bolt. There were footsteps on the stairs. Mo had picked up the lavatory brush and was holding it as if it was an offensive weapon. I dashed to the window and pulled it up. Someone tried the door handle.

"Come on," I hissed at Mo.

Three feet below the window is the roof of the kitchen, which is a single-storey extension tacked on to the main house. I threw out the rucksack. It rolled down the slope of the roof, teetered for a moment on the gutter and then vanished.

"We are police officers," Trubshaw said on the other side of the door. "Open the door and no harm will come to you."

"Crap," said Mo. She dived through the window and landed painfully on the ridge of the slates. She was clambering down to the guttering as I followed her through the window.

I glanced back as I left. A panel of the bathroom door splintered inwards. A large hand with black-rimmed nails poked through the gap.

"It's a bloody kid," Pete said.

The slates were rough and warm from the sun. I slithered downwards on my bottom. Mo was already on the ground. I jumped from the roof on to the water butt and from there to the grass.

Mo was running down the garden with my rucksack on her arm. She realized that the back door would be locked. In any case the house was a trap. I ran after her.

Our garden's about eighty feet long. Most of it's jungle because my mum thinks that the best thing to do in a garden is to sit in it. The jungle ends in an old brick wall. A gate in the wall opens on to an alley which runs between the back gardens of our road and those of the next road along.

At the gate I looked back. A bloke with silver hair and a natty grey suit was leaning out of the bathroom window. Trubshaw, I thought. The other bloke, Pete, was in the act of jumping from the roof to the water butt. I caught a glimpse of his face: he looked like Frankenstein's monster, cast in iron. The cover of the butt gave way beneath his weight.

I sprinted down the path. I could hear him swearing. I wondered what Mrs Jones would make of it.

The alley runs straight as a ruler for about two hundred yards. It comes out in a side road near the station. Mo paused there, waiting for me to come up. Her face was grim.

I glanced back and saw why. Iron-Face Pete was pounding after us. His wet trousers slapped against his legs. Trubshaw puffed along behind him.

"Quick," Mo said. "We'll lose them at the station."

Unfortunately Iron-Face could run. We heard his heavy boots thudding down the road behind us. In my mind the sound got confused with the beating of my heart, which was trying to escape from my chest.

The railway station has a U-shaped approach road which slopes down to the station entrance at the bottom of the U. People were pouring out – a train must have just arrived. A queue of taxis was waiting for them.

Mo yanked open the door of the nearest cab.

"Oy," the driver said. "You wait your turn like everyone else."

"Oh please," Mo said. "It's our mother. We've got to get

to the Infirmary. She may be dying."

Mo opened her eyes as widely as she could. Her voice had changed too. I've seen her do this before: she goes all girlish and pathetic and appealing, as though she was applying for a part in *The Sound of Music*. It's surprising how often it works with adults who don't know her.

"All right," the bloke said. "Hop in."

We were already inside. Iron-Face was no more than thirty yards away.

"I hope you've got some money," the cabby went on. "I'm not a blooming charity."

I pulled out the ten pound note and waved it at him.

"Please hurry," Mo pleaded. "Every second counts." She began to sob realistically into a paper handkerchief.

The driver let out the clutch and pulled away.

I glanced back. Iron-Face was trying to grab another taxi. He wasn't having much success. It looked like the queue was about to turn into a lynch mob.

We paid off the taxi at the Royal Infirmary. It's in the middle of the town so it was easy to get a bus back to Mo's. We were certain that Trubshaw and Iron-Face hadn't been able to follow us.

In the bus we sat on top at the front. Both of us were still panting. I had the rucksack on my lap. Like a snail I was carrying my home. Mo poked me in the ribs.

"I wonder if they were," she said.

"If who were what?"

"Coppers. I mean, they said they were."

"But surely . . ." My voice trailed away. Nothing was sure any more.

"Maybe your mum was involved with the heroin," Mo said. "Accidentally, like. Maybe the police asked your dad to get them a key."

"I don't believe it," I said stubbornly.

I knew Davis wasn't a drug-pusher. And I knew he wouldn't involve Mum even if he was.

Mo shrugged. "OK. Just an idea."

We didn't talk for the rest of the journey. I looked at my watch when we got back to Mo's. It was only eleven. It felt like we'd been away for days.

Mo's mum was out shopping. We had the flat to ourselves. We were starving again so I cooked us baked beans on toast. The toast got burnt and the baked beans stuck to the bottom of the saucepan.

Afterwards we sat around in Mo's room, listening to a tape and trying to decide what to do next. It wasn't easy. I found it hard to concentrate because I was wondering where I was going to sleep that night. I doubted if Mo's parents would offer to put me up.

The conversation fizzled out. I could tell that Mo was itching to try the disc she'd borrowed from Mum. In the end she switched on her computer. It used to belong to her brother – he gave it to her last Christmas when he bought a better one. She loaded the disc and started fiddling with her keyboard.

I was on the verge of drowning in self-pity. Even Mo didn't give a damn that I was about to become a homeless waif. I took out Davis's postcard. Auntie Mabel indeed. That man has a weird sense of humour. I wondered if he was certifiable.

It occurred to me that Auntie Mabel might be more than a joke. Mum and I know we haven't got an Auntie Mabel, but anyone else who saw the postcard would think it was on the level. Suppose Davis had no other way of getting in touch?

I began to think hard. If the postcard wasn't a joke, Davis must have had another reason for sending it. Perhaps he didn't sign his real name because he already knew the police were after him.

But why didn't he stay to prove his innocence? Either because he was guilty, which I wouldn't believe, or because he could only prove his innocence by going away. By going to Easton.

Maybe he and Mum had arranged about the postcard beforehand? No, that wouldn't work. Mum had definitely been expecting Davis to supper last night. There was meat in the casserole and she hardly ever cooks meat unless he's going to be there. It looked as though Davis had written the postcard as a last resort – when he knew he wouldn't be able to come to our house.

Why a postcard when he could have phoned? I thought about that for a while and came up with the idea that maybe he had tried to phone – after Mum left the house and before I came back. I wondered if that meant he'd been on his way to somewhere that wasn't on the telephone. Of course he might have tried again later in the evening after Dad had taken me away.

All these ifs and maybes were making me dizzy. It was guesswork. I turned back to the postcard. At least that was real. I studied the photos. I reread the message from Auntie Mabel. I even read the caption at the bottom:

"EASTON-ON-SEA. The West Pier (1893). The Imperial Spa Hotel. Children's Playground in the Bracknell Memorial Gardens. The Gannet's Head and Sea Panorama."

The Gannet's Head? The cliffs looked more like a pile of rocks to me. I stared at the squiggles that Davis had made on the bottom of the card. There was something odd about them. You know what happens when you're trying to make a biro work? At first it makes a mark on the paper but no ink comes out. Then the ink gradually begins to flow.

But on Davis's postcard the ink had been flowing all the time. If he hadn't been trying to make his biro work, what had he been doing?

I found a pencil on Mo's table and copied out some of the letters in the caption – the ones which had been touched by the squiggles. My heart sank when I saw the result:

S . . .NO . . . m . . i . . S . . .ot . . .e . . .n . . .o . . .
G . . .r . . . .e . . .G . . .n . . . .ad.

"Snomi sot eno Greg nad?" I said experimentally. Saying it aloud didn't make it sound clearer. "Snom isoten ogre gnad?" I wondered if Davis had been doing evening classes in Russian or Esperanto.

"Eh?" Mo looked away from her screen. "What's that?"

"You tell me. I thought maybe it was a message from Davis. But if it is, it's in code or in a foreign language."

31

I pushed the postcard and my bit of paper across the table. Mo looked at it for about two seconds. Then she burst out laughing.

"You're so thick sometimes. Honestly, Sam. All he did was write it backwards."

" 'Danger,' " I read aloud. " 'Gone to Simon's.' "

Mo stopped laughing.

"Two halves to Easton, please."

"Single or return?" the ticket clerk said.

That floored me for a moment. We had to be careful about how much we spent. I didn't know whether I'd be coming back or not.

Mo elbowed me aside. "Returns."

"Reduced service tomorrow," the clerk said mechanically. "Emergency engineering work on the line. No trains at all after four p.m."

"That's OK," Mo said. "We're coming back today."

Unlike me, Mo's good at making decisions. Of course she needed a return: she had a home to go to. I fumbled with the money and managed to drop the change the clerk gave me. I couldn't help thinking that no one was going to worry about where I was tonight.

We went on to the station concourse, keeping our eyes skinned for Trubshaw and Iron-Face. There was no reason for them to be here but both of us were wary after what had happened this morning.

The concourse is like a great big iron cathedral. It was crowded with people who'd come into the city to do their Saturday shopping. Pigeons were flying dive-bombing sorties overhead.

A couple of policemen were wandering around. They did nothing for my peace of mind. Even if Trubshaw and Iron-Face weren't plain-clothes men, cops were bad news. They were after Davis. Sooner or later Dad would set them after me.

We were lucky: an Easton train was due to leave in five minutes' time at 12.57. It was one of these little local trains with three carriages, the sort that look like they want to be a family of buses when they grow up. We bought some chocolate to eat on the way.

Mo was not in the best of moods. She'd run into a problem with the disc she'd borrowed from our house. She kept muttering about limbo files and kilobytes and stuff like that. She'd even brought the disc with her. It was in the pocket of the light jacket that lay on the seat between us.

"You're sure that Simon's got the same computer?" she asked for the umpteenth time.

"I've told you," I said wearily. "All I know is that me and my mother and Davis were going to stay at his cottage for a week before school starts. And I heard Davis telling Mum that her discs would work on his computer so she could bring some games."

"Games," Mo said scornfully. "Kids' stuff. How far's the cottage from Easton?"

"I don't know. I've only been there once and that was by car. Five or ten miles, maybe."

Simon's cottage is on a hill overlooking the estuary. It's in the middle of nowhere. His nearest neighbour is a quarter of a mile away. If all else failed, we'd have to get another taxi.

By now the train was crawling down the estuary. It was another hot, sweaty day but it was a lot cooler now we were moving. The windows were open and you could sometimes see the sea. The train stopped at all the little stations on the way. Sometimes no one got out and no one got on. It was almost like we had our own private train.

"And who is Simon, anyway?" Mo asked.

"Friend of Davis's. He's another journalist."

"Will he be there? Can we trust him?"

I shook my head. "Simon's in Africa on a story this summer. That's why Davis is looking after his cottage."

"Funny place for a journalist to live." Mo snorted: she's a city person. "And how does he manage without a phone?"

"Oh, he doesn't live there all the time. It's a sort of

weekend cottage."

"He must be filthy rich." Mo sounded envious.

"Davis says he's sold out and joined the establishment."

Mo pulled a face. "I'd sell out if anyone would buy me."

The train rattled on. I stared out of the window, wondering if Davis really was at Simon's and worrying about my mother. At times like this, I decided, there's only one way to keep from going insane: you have to take one step at a time. First we had to get to Simon's. There was no point in worrying about anything else until we got there. It was good advice. But it's easier to think of good advice than to put it into practice.

We pulled up at another little station. I tried to distract myself by watching the seagulls. Quite a lot of people got out of the carriage next to ours. Suddenly Mo sucked in her breath.

"Look," she said.

She was pointing out of the window at the platform. I couldn't see what she was on about. All you could see was a perfectly ordinary railway station. A railway official was leaning against the wall, picking his teeth. The train juddered and began to pull away.

"See where we are?" Mo said.

I just had time to catch the name of the station as the train picked up speed.

"Histon . . ." Mo tugged her ear. "That's what Trubshaw told Iron-Face to look for. Any papers with Magnox or Histon written on them."

It's funny but I was almost sorry when we reached Easton. I'd got used to the train. It seemed safe. Outside, everything was unknown.

Mo hustled me out of the station. I had a bad moment when I realized that I didn't even know the name of the nearest village to Simon's cottage. Mo solved that problem. She marched up to a policeman and demanded the way to the tourist office.

It was on the seafront near the pier on the postcard. The

beach was knee-deep in pink and peeling people of all ages. The fast-food stalls were doing a roaring trade. Kids were splashing in the sea. Farther out, you could see windsurfers and water-skiers. Everyone seemed to be shouting or playing their radios at full blast. What right had they to enjoy themselves? For an instant I wished they'd all get sunstroke or be enveloped by a tidal wave.

The tourist office was packed. Mo burrowed through the crowd to a big map of the area that hung on one wall. I followed in her wake.

I knew the cottage couldn't be far from the estuary and that behind it there was a large wooded hill with some sort of prehistoric earthwork on top. There aren't many patches of wood on our side of the estuary and only one of them was marked "Iron Age Fort".

The nearest village was a place called Gorbury. We must have passed quite close to it on the train. It was roughly halfway between Easton and Histon.

According to the symbols on the map, Gorbury wasn't much more than a public house and a church with a square tower. Behind it, the land rose sharply towards the fort. On the lower slopes of the hill were a few scattered black blobs, one of which must be Simon's cottage.

Mo fought her way to the counter and came back with the information that the next bus to Gorbury was at 3.45, nearly two hours away. It was an half-hour journey. There wouldn't be a bus back until six.

"That's torn it," I said.

"Why?"

"If you come with me to Gorbury, you won't get home till late. The train takes nearly an hour."

Mo shrugged. "Sometimes," she drawled, "you gotta live dangerously." She added in her normal voice: "Maybe I should try and phone our neighbour – leave a message for my parents. I'll say I'm spending the night with a friend."

I tried to hide my relief. "Won't they mind?"

"My mum and dad? You must be joking." Mo stared

out to sea. "Sometimes I think they'd rather I wasn't there at all."

Neither of us said anything for a moment. My mother goes spare if I stay out later than I said I would. When you're young, you think all parents are like your own. When you get older, you start comparing notes with your friends. For a moment I stopped feeling sorry for myself and felt sorry for Mo instead.

We walked along the promenade, looking for a phone box. We passed several but all of them were either occupied or vandalized. Mo was getting angrier and angrier.

At the end of the promenade was a big white hotel which looked rather like an overgrown wedding cake. As we drew nearer I realized it was the Imperial Spa, the one on Davis's postcard.

Mo nodded towards the hotel. "They'll have a pay-phone," she said airily. "You coming with me?"

"You can't go in there," I said. "They'll chuck you out."

"Want to bet? If anyone stops me, I'll talk posh and say my parents are having luncheon there."

She crossed the forecourt and climbed the steps to the main entrance. There was a doorman in a chocolate-brown coat and a matching top hat. On a day like this he must have been boiling.

Mo glared at him. He opened the door for her. I nearly cheered.

I stayed on the promenade. The Imperial Spa had a gravelled forecourt. I counted two Rolls-Royces and three Mercedes parked there. It was that sort of hotel.

The sun and lack of sleep were getting to me. I hunkered down, leaning back against the wall separating the prom- enade from the beach. My eyelids began to droop. Sud- denly I jerked awake.

A white Bentley was purring along the road. As I watched, it turned into the hotel forecourt. Something clicked in my mind: the big white car that Mrs Jones saw and the Bentley outside my father's flat last night. There couldn't be that many white Bentleys in this area.

The doorman had seen the car too. He practically fell down the steps in his eagerness to reach it. He opened the driver's door with a flourish. I thought he was going to kneel down on the gravel.

The driver got out. As soon as I saw his head, my hopes sank. The man who visited Dad's flat had red-gold hair; this bloke's hair was white.

But I didn't stop watching because the driver looked so odd. He was a small man, not much bigger than me or Mo. But he had huge arms and shoulders. As he came round the car, I saw that the rest of his body tapered down to a small waist, short legs and tiny feet. He looked like a triangle turned upside down.

That makes him sound like a bit of a joke. I haven't mentioned his face yet and that's where the joke turned sour. His features were blurred, as if someone had gone over them with heavy-duty sandpaper. The skin was coloured an angry red. What you immediately noticed were the eyes, even from where I was. They were a bright, uncomfortable blue.

OK, I thought, he's weird but he's nothing to do with me.

Then the door on the passenger side opened. A tall, overweight man hauled himself out of the car. He stood there for an instant, panting as though he'd just run a race. He looked exactly like a toad in a pinstripe suit. A shiver zoomed up my spine.

The passenger was Giles Viney, my mother's boss in the planning department.

I rested my head on my hands and peeped through my fingers. It was best to play safe though I doubted if Viney would recognize me. We'd met briefly in Mum's office. But I got the impression he hadn't really registered me, if you know what I mean. Viney's the sort of person who only notices you if he thinks you can do something for him.

The two men went up the flight of steps. Viney mopped

his face with a handkerchief. The doorman scurried ahead to open the door. Just as he got there, it opened from the inside.

Mo came out. She looked snootily at the doorman and strolled down the steps as if she owned the place. She walked straight between Viney and the dwarf, forcing them to move aside. Apart from that, neither of them seemed to notice her.

The two men vanished into the hotel. Mo reached the bottom of the steps and gave me a thumbs-up sign: so she'd managed to use a phone. She waited for a moment at the bottom of the steps because a taxi had just come into the forecourt. I caught a glimpse of the two passengers in the back.

Suddenly the smile was wiped off Mo's face. She started to run. Not across the road to me but back along the promenade in the direction we'd come from.

Someone sprang out of the taxi and ran after her. A second later I realized it wasn't just any old someone.

It was Iron-Face Pete.

Trubshaw paid off the taxi and hurried up the steps into the Imperial Spa.

I looked along the stretch of the promenade. I could see Iron-Face lumbering along but there was no sign of Mo's red T-shirt. She must have turned off. The question was, where? On to the beach or into the town? At least she had a better idea of the layout of Easton than I did.

At any moment Trubshaw would be back with reinforcements. If I followed Mo along the promenade, I'd run into Iron-Face. Without giving myself time to think, I grabbed the rucksack, pulled myself up on to the wall and jumped down to the beach.

"What the hell d'you think you're doing?" an old woman barked.

It was a fair question. I'd landed in the middle of a picnic. Two toddlers were looking up at me with open mouths full of sandwich. The old woman, the toddlers' gran maybe, had faster reactions: she'd already grabbed one of the kid's spades and was waving it in my direction. She was obviously the sort who believes that actions speak louder than words.

I backed away from her. The toddlers screwed up their faces. Their screams emptied their mouths. Bits of sandwich bounced off my legs.

"Sorry," I muttered.

I dodged away across the beach. It was so crowded I felt safe. As well as people on their summer holidays, there were lots of day-trippers from the city. Scores of kids were running around, so I wasn't conspicuous.

The beach is divided by breakwaters. I paused in the shelter of one of them, down by the edge of the water. I stared up at the promenade.

The feeling of safety vanished. I could see the whole frontage of the Imperial Spa – everything except for the ground floor. The sun flashed on the big windows behind the hotel's balconies. Viney could be standing there, along with the white-haired bloke with the Bentley. Maybe they were sweeping the beach with binoculars.

OK, so my imagination was working double overtime. In this case it was just as well. If I hadn't been looking back, I wouldn't have seen Trubshaw.

He was standing at the head of a flight of steps which led down from the promenade. As I watched, he walked slowly down to the beach. I swung myself over the breakwater and ducked behind it. A few yards away, a middle-aged couple were sunning themselves in the sand like a pair of pink porpoises. They stared curiously at me. I ignored them and peered cautiously over the top of the breakwater.

Trubshaw was in the wrong place at the wrong time. Practically everyone on the beach was half-naked and having fun. Trubshaw looked as if he belonged on another planet. There he was in a dark suit, with a white shirt and a natty striped tie. I couldn't see his shoes but I knew they'd be gleaming with polish.

He wasn't in a hurry. He walked down to the sea's edge and back to the promenade. Then he repeated the process, again and again. Every zigzag was bringing him closer to me.

There was something coldly methodical about his search. His boss had obviously told him to check the beach, in case Mo had slipped down there. It was more than likely that Trubshaw was also looking for me. He and Iron-Face had seen me and Mo together this morning: they'd expect me to be here.

For an instant I was tempted to run – either along the beach in front of him or up to the promenade. But either way I could end up running into the arms of Iron-Face.

"It beats me," the female porpoise said suddenly, "how

you can keep out of the water on a day like this. My boys loved the sea when they were your age."

It took me a moment to realize that she was talking to me.

"Now, now, dear," said the male porpoise mildly. "Perhaps he doesn't want to go swimming."

"Of course he does." The woman's voice was brisk. She looked up at me. "Don't you?"

Well, why not, I thought? The sea looked incredibly inviting. More importantly, one body in the water is pretty much like any other. You couldn't ask for a better place to hide. My underpants were enough like swimming trunks for it not to matter. Mr and Mrs Porpoise could keep an eye on my things.

I pulled off my clothes and stuffed them in the rucksack. I ran through the shallows to the deeper water beyond. The sea felt great: all the heat of the day and half my worries seemed to drop away from me. For a few seconds I was almost happy.

At first I swam round in circles, watching Trubshaw. When he got closer, I swam further out, turned on my back and floated. He couldn't have been able to see much more than my toes and the tip of my nose. I counted up to three hundred. When I next looked, Trubshaw was past my breakwater and walking up the beach again.

I swam closer to the beach and lay in the shallows. Little waves ran over my back. Mr and Mrs Porpoise were packing up their things. When they went, Mrs P gave me a wave.

My relief slowly ebbed away and I started feeling guilty. I was safe – for the moment – but what about Mo? I told myself there was nothing I could do to help her, which was true. That didn't make me feel any less guilty. I splashed out of the sea and lay down on the sand to get dry.

I reckoned the best thing to do was to stay on the beach for another hour. If I was careful, I should be able to keep a watch on the promenade and avoid Trubshaw and Iron-Face. I wanted to find Mo, of course, but I also wanted to see what happened to the white Bentley. After the hour was up, I'd head for the bus station. That was where Mo would go. If she could.

My mind went back to the Bentley. It was funny how it seemed to turn up everywhere. I wondered if the little man who drove it was the one Iron-Face had called "Hairy". But if he was Hairy, who was Dad's visitor last night? I just couldn't believe it wasn't the same Bentley.

Suddenly a spray of sand hit my face. I gasped and looked up.

You know those Charles Atlas adverts where the bully kicks sand in the skinny bloke's face? It was just like that, with me playing the part of the victim.

The bully was Roland.

He was looming over me, flexing his muscles. Since yesterday afternoon, he'd had his hair cut and styled. Our Roland's a bit of a dandy. Even his swimming trunks were black and gold, with a fancy monogram. As our eyes met, he smiled as though someone had unexpectedly given him a present.

"Well, well," he said. "Look who it isn't."

It was funny but Roland seemed to have shrunk since I last saw him. He just wasn't in the same league as Trubshaw and Iron-Face. But he was still quite capable of beating me up. And a full-scale fight would be sure to attract attention.

I licked my lips and gave him a polite smile. "Hello, Roland."

As I spoke I tried to lever myself up. A bare foot slammed into my shoulder and drove me back against the breakwater.

"You look kinda like a doormat," he drawled. "So I'm gonna wipe my feet on you."

Roland's attempts to talk like a gangster would be funny if he didn't have a nasty habit of meaning exactly what he says. The foot came down again and rested on my face.

At times like that you don't bother with the Queensberry rules. I wrapped my mouth around the edge of his foot and bit as hard as I could.

Roland yelled. He hopped backwards and tripped over the

remains of a sand castle.

I leapt to my feet and scooped up the rucksack. Roland was pulling himself out of the shallows. It isn't easy to sprint on loose sand and shingle but I did my best.

As I ran up the beach I had two thoughts in my head: one, that I seemed to be spending most of my life running away from people; and two, that I'd left my wet shoe drying out on top of the breakwater.

A second later, a third thought pushed the other two out of my mind. Roland was after me. I glanced back and there he was, twenty yards behind. His body glistened with water, his hair was all messed up and his face was puffy with rage.

That glance was an expensive luxury. I ran into a man coming the other way. Roland halved my lead because of it.

I swerved away from him. The retaining wall of the promenade was directly in front of me. At this point it was four or five feet high. The nearest steps were fifty yards away. I grabbed the top and hoisted myself up. The rough stone grated against my bare skin.

The Imperial Spa was almost in front of me.

My legs were still dangling over the beach. Roland grabbed one of my feet. I kicked backwards and wriggled violently. The next thing I knew, I was sprawling on the promenade.

There was no time to waste. Roland's head and shoulders were already above the level of the wall. I scrambled to my feet. That was when I saw Trubshaw again.

He was maybe a hundred yards up the promenade and coming towards me. He was looking over the beach and I didn't think he'd seen me. But if I ran towards the town centre, I'd run slap into him. If I stayed to fight Roland, Trubshaw could hardly avoid noticing.

I took a few steps in the other direction. There was a man ahead and I was suddenly convinced that he looked familiar. It's Iron-Face, I thought, they'll trap me between them.

To this day I don't know if it really was Iron-Face. When you're desperate, you don't think straight. You don't do much thinking at all. You just act.

I darted across the road. Brakes shrieked. Drivers blew

their horns. I deserved to get myself killed, and God knows why I didn't.

Roland was close behind. I had no time to think, no room for manoeuvre. Gravel savaged the soles of my feet: I was running up the drive of the Imperial Spa. I knew it was a stupid thing to do. All I could think of was that Roland might not have the guts to follow me, and that if Trubshaw and Iron-Face hadn't recognized me outside, the hotel was the last place where they'd look for me.

"Hey!" the doorman shouted. "You!"

I ducked under his arm and burst through the swing door into the hotel foyer. Roland ran straight into the doorman and bounced off. They swore at one another and then Roland retreated to the road. He stood on the pavement, waiting for me to get chucked out.

The doorman, his face grim, came in to get me.

I suddenly realized how I must look. I was wearing nothing except sodden underpants and a layer of damp sand; I was clutching a rucksack and panting like a dog. People were staring at me. There was a buzz of hostile whispering. I suppose they didn't see someone like me very often in the Imperial Spa.

I felt very tired. This was the end of the road. The doorman was going to throw me out. Then Roland would beat the hell out of me and leave what was left for Trubshaw and Iron-Face to scrape off the pavement.

The doorman grabbed my ear and twisted it.

"Now, kiddo," he said – softly, because there were guests around. "If I see you round here again, you'll get a damn sight worse than a thick ear. On your bike."

"It's all right, Michael," someone said from the stairs. "You can let him go."

The doorman swung round. "Begging your pardon, sir, this kid's a bloody menace."

"I know," my father said. "He's also my son."

CHAPTER SEVEN

The Queen Victoria Suite was at the front of the hotel, directly above the foyer. The furniture looked as if it had been gold-plated. French windows opened on to a balcony overlooking the sea front.

I wasn't looking at the furnishings or the view. I was looking at the man behind the desk. My father was standing beside me. Giles Viney sat by one of the windows, fidgeting with a long-stemmed glass in his hand. My father had made me wash and get dressed. He'd also bought me a pair of trainers at one of the hotel shops.

The man behind the desk stared back at me. It was the bloke with the Bentley. Sitting down, he looked much bigger – you noticed the size of the shoulders, not the puny little legs. Now I was closer, I could see that the angry skin on his face was seamed with lines like a patchwork quilt.

His cold, blue eyes were making me feel uncomfortable but I wasn't going to be the first to look away. I wouldn't give him that advantage. I realized that one reason why the eyes seemed so piercing was that they hadn't any lashes. He hadn't any eyebrows either.

Beside me, Dad shifted his weight from one foot to the other.

"I'm sorry about this, Mr Witcham," he said. "Sam just appeared downstairs. Some kid was chasing him."

Witcham's eyes flicked across to Dad and then back to me. It was as though he'd decided that Dad wasn't worth looking at.

"Sam," he said slowly. "I had a daughter once. She would have been about your age. Well, well, well."

His voice came as another surprise. It was high and soft like a woman's.

Viney stirred in his chair. "Victor, I hate to hurry you. But the TV crew will be here at any moment."

Witcham glanced across the room at him and then back to me.

"I'm so glad you've found us," he said. "We've all been looking for you, you know. Your father was so worried he couldn't concentrate, could you, Mark? By the way, Sam, where's your little friend?"

Suddenly I was angry. "Where's my mother?"

Dad grabbed my arm. "Sam – "

Witcham shut him up with a wave of his hand. "I'm afraid I can't help you," he said to me. "I think your father mentioned that she's having a little holiday."

"I've explained all that to him," my father said.

"Of course you have, Mark." Witcham's voice lost its softness. "And I expect you've checked Sam's pockets and his rucksack?"

Dad nodded. "No luck, I'm afraid."

There was a knock on the door, and Trubshaw and Iron-Face came in. They did a double take when they saw me standing there; so they couldn't have seen me on the promenade. Trubshaw looked at Witcham and gave a tiny shake of his head. I hoped that meant they hadn't caught Mo.

"They're here," Viney said. He stood up and peered over the balcony. "One big van and a couple of cars."

My father cleared his throat. "What are we going to do with Sam?"

Witcham looked at me again. He was frowning slightly. I wasn't a person as far as he was concerned – just a problem that need solving.

"Put him next door," he said at last. "It's a bedroom, isn't it?"

"But Mr Witcham – " Dad began.

"Not for long, Mark, don't worry." Witcham bared his teeth in what might have been intended as a reassuring smile. "I'm sure Trubshaw will look after him."

Trubshaw put his hand on my shoulder. "I'll take care of everything, Mr Witcham. You can rely on me." He sounded like he was pretending to be a butler in an old film.

"All right, Mark?" Witcham said. "It won't be for long."

"Yes, of course," Dad said feebly. "I quite understand."

This can't be happening, I thought. This man's meant to be my father.

Trubshaw hustled me through a door behind Witcham's desk. At close quarters he stank of aftershave. There was a little passage with a bathroom opening off it. The bedroom was at the far end. He shoved me through the door.

Iron-Face followed us in with my rucksack dangling over his arm. He threw it on the bed.

"One down," he said, "and one to go."

Trubshaw looked down his nose at him. "No thanks to you. We've got to find that girl." He swung round and grabbed my arm. "What's her name?"

When I said nothing, he shook me like a cat shakes a mouse.

"And where's she got to?" he asked.

Another silence; another shake.

Iron-Face Pete grunted. "You want me to make him talk?"

His tone was casual, as though he was asking Trubshaw if he wanted some coffee. But he was offering to torture me.

Trubshaw shook his head. "Better not," he said regretfully. "In the circumstances we need to get clearance. Perhaps later."

They had a whispered conversation which I couldn't hear. Then both of them took off their ties. Trubshaw held me while Iron-Face knotted one round my wrists and the other round my ankles. Iron-Face fetched a hand towel from the bathroom. He stuffed most of it in my mouth and pushed me backwards on to the bed.

Trubshaw locked the door we had come through. Iron-Face was standing by the other door. I guessed it led to the corridor outside the suite.

"Sweet dreams," Trubshaw said.

I was alone. The key turned in the lock. I reckoned they were going to look for Mo again.

As soon as their footsteps had died away, I was wriggling

towards my rucksack. I knew my father had been through the contents while I was getting dressed, presumably looking for whatever it was that Trubshaw and Iron-Face had failed to find at our house. I was banking on the possibility that he hadn't taken the imitation Swiss Army penknife from the side pocket.

It was still there. I could feel it through the thick nylon. I fumbled at the buckle for ages. The strap was stiff and I couldn't see what I was doing. My hands grew sticky with sweat. You try undoing a buckle when you're lying on your side on a soft bed with your hands tied behind your back.

I got the pocket open at last and pulled out the knife. The next problem was opening the blade. My fingers kept slipping. At one point I got cramp which forced me to stop for a moment.

But the worst part was when I tried to cut through the tie. It was almost impossible to keep the blade steady. I cut myself twice in the process. As I sawed away I was muttering aloud: hurry, hurry, hurry.

The tie gave way. I sat up, groaning and massaging my wrists. There were drops of blood on the sky blue bedspread. I hacked through the other tie, swung my legs off the bed and stood up. Only then did I realize that I hadn't the faintest idea what I was going to do.

If I banged on the door, someone would eventually come. So would my father. He'd apologize again for his problem son and I'd be back to square one.

I opened the French window and went out on to the balcony. I had a vague idea of shouting for help. I knew it wouldn't be much use in the long run but at least it would embarrass my father and Witcham.

The balcony overlooked the beach. Roland was still on the promenade. He'd got dressed and was smoking a cigarette while he kept an eye on the hotel. On my left were the French windows of the big sitting room where Witcham and Co were holed up with the television crew. On the right was a high brick wall. I leant round it and saw that the balcony continued along the front of the hotel.

I strapped on the rucksack and pulled myself up on to the handrail. It was wrought iron and hot to the touch. Edging round the partition was one of the worst things I've ever had to do.

It wasn't just the fear of falling, bad though that was. Immediately below me was an iron railing like a row of spears. I could imagine what they'd do to me if I slipped.

There were other things to be afraid of. Witcham or someone might come out on the balcony. Roland might look up and see me. And in a few seconds I'd have to face whatever was on the other side of the partition.

The next balcony was empty. I jumped down from the rail and just stood there for a moment. I was shaking. This balcony was smaller than the one I'd just left because it belonged to a bedroom, not a whole suite. The French window was ajar. A towel and a bikini were drying on the handrail.

The bedroom was gloomy after the brightness of the balcony. I couldn't see anyone in there but the shower was hissing in the bathroom. I tiptoed across the carpet towards the door.

Suddenly the shower stopped.

"Is that room service?" a woman's voice demanded. "Just leave the tea on the table."

I ran for the door and burst out into the corridor. Just as I closed the door, a maid carrying a tea tray came out of the lift. I sauntered past her, whistling casually to show I had every right to be here. She glanced sharply at me. Maybe people weren't supposed to whistle in the Imperial Spa.

I still had to get out of the hotel. My father might check on me. Trubshaw and Iron-Face could be back at any time. At first I was going to stroll down the stairs and out of the front door. I changed my mind when I got to the head of the stairs. Michael the doorman was down there, chatting up the receptionist. Even if I could get past him, Roland was waiting for me outside.

The maid came out of the room I'd just left. This time she looked at me with open suspicion. That's how it seemed to me, anyway. I turned into a side corridor to avoid her.

This part of the corridor led to the back of the hotel. At the far end was a red door. Above it was an illuminated sign: FIRE EXIT.

I ran down to the door. You opened it by pushing a horizontal bar. I grabbed it and shoved.

"What do you think you're doing?"

It was the maid. She probably thought I was a burglar. And it looked like she was keen to make a citizen's arrest.

The door opened with a jerk. I stumbled on to the fire escape and plunged down it, three steps at a time. At the bottom was a shabby yard crammed with dustbins. Even at the time I remember thinking how different the back of the hotel was from the front.

There was a gate on the other side of the yard. I tugged it open and glanced back. The maid had come out on the fire escape. She saw me looking up and started to scream for help.

I found myself in a long straight road which was lined with small hotels and boarding houses. I'd never been there before but I guessed it must run parallel to the promenade. So if I turned right I'd reach the town centre sooner or later.

I hoped it would be sooner because there wasn't much time. I glanced at my watch as I ran down the road. It was already 3.35 – the bus to Gorbury would be leaving in ten minutes. Now, more than ever, I had to find Davis. I knew that Victor Witcham was somehow concerned with Mum's disappearance. I knew Viney and Dad were mixed up with him. I knew who. Maybe Davis would know why.

I reached the bus station with a minute to spare. The Gorbury bus already had its engine running. But I didn't get on board. It was one of those single-decker buses with the only door at the front. Once I got on, I'd be trapped. Trubshaw and Iron-Face were on the loose. I wasn't taking any unnecessary chances. That was one lesson I'd learned in the last twenty-four hours.

The bus was already quite full. I walked round it but Mo wasn't on board. That worried me sick.

I knew she'd have got here if she could. The most likely explanation was that Trubshaw and Iron-Face had managed to find her first. There wasn't a thing I could do about it.

The bus driver revved the engine. I realized it was time to go. A fat man heaved himself on board. I climbed in after him and bought my ticket.

Most of the seats were taken but there were two empty ones side by side near the back. The bus started to move as I followed the fat man down the gangway. We were obviously making for the same seats. I wondered if there would be any room for me once he'd sat down.

"Excuse me," said the fat man. "I'd like to sit down. You can't take up two seats."

Mo's head appeared above the seat backs.

"I'm keeping this seat for a friend," she said. "Look, he's just behind you."

CHAPTER EIGHT

"If I don't have something to drink," Mo announced as we walked down the one street of the village, "I'm going to die. Probably in about ten minutes."

"You've picked the right place," I said.

It was stupid thing to say but in a way it was true. Gorbury was the deadest place I'd ever seen. We were the only people who got off the bus. No one was around. Not even a net curtain twitched in a cottage window. The pub had a sign saying it was closed for repairs. The one shop was shut. None of the gravestones in the churchyard looked as if it was much younger than a hundred years.

Mo plodded along behind me, muttering under her breath. She was exhausted. She'd spent most of the afternoon playing hide-and-seek with Trubshaw and Iron-Face. At one point Iron-Face nearly caught her. But he wasn't quite brave enough to follow her into the ladies' loo on the promenade. And he couldn't be expected to know that the ladies' loo has two entrances.

I could have done with a drink myself. It was still hot and the last thing I wanted to do was to go for a country walk. To make matters worse I couldn't even be sure we were walking in the right direction. The other time I'd been here, I'd only glimpsed the village and that was from a car. Things look a lot different when you're on foot.

I had the sense not to mention my doubts to Mo. Three roads led out of the village. I just picked the one signposted Histon and set off. I wanted to get out of Gorbury as soon as possible. Strangers stand out in villages and we didn't want to be conspicuous. I'd have felt safer in the city.

I think Mo had the same idea in her mind. We heard a car coming in the opposite direction. Without a word both of us plunged into the ditch. A police car, one of those tiddly Ford Fiestas, drove past. There were two uniformed coppers inside.

We stood up. I was feeling rather stupid.

Mo stared after the car and sighed. "I wish we knew whose side we're supposed to be on."

Outside the village the road began to climb. There was a sharp bend and the wooded hill came into view. A lane went off towards it on the left. I recognized the turn-off because there was a postbox on the corner. I'd guessed the right road.

I stopped by the postbox and waited for Mo to catch up. The trees covered the prehistoric hill fort like a thick green fog. Under a clear blue sky and in full sunlight it managed to look sinister.

The lane was winding and narrow. It ran between high, untrimmed hedges. We hadn't gone far when we heard a clanking sound coming towards us.

Mo looked at me and we shrugged. This time there was nowhere to hide. The hedges were as effective as stone walls. We could have run back down the hill, I suppose, but I think we both thought we'd done enough running for one day.

The clanking grew louder as we walked towards it. We came round a hairpin bend and ran into the glare of the sinking sun. For an instant I could barely see. Two huge people were no more than ten yards away.

Beside me, Mo giggled. She turned the sound quickly into a cough.

I shaded my eyes and discovered that the newcomers weren't that much bigger than us. They just seemed that way because each of them was carrying a large frame rucksack. The clanking was caused by the cooking equipment tied to the frames.

"You go to yewt ostelle?" the taller one demanded.

I stared at him without understanding. He and his friend wore sweatshirts, sandals and very short shorts. I wouldn't wear shorts like that if you paid me a fortune.

Mo's mind moved faster than mine. "*Vous êtes Français*?"

Then we all started talking at once in a mixture of French

and English, with a lot of sign language thrown in. We gathered that their names were Philippe and André, and that they were on a camping holiday here. They assumed we were heading for the youth hostel near Histon because of my rucksack. We let them go on thinking that.

They warned us that there was no longer a short cut to the hostel. They pulled out their map and showed us a footpath which zigzagged over the hill and then across some open fields to the hostel on the outskirts of Histon village.

The problem was, the fields had been fenced in. There were notices about trespassing and a bull was in one of the fields. The footpath had disappeared. As a result, they'd have to walk to the hostel by road, which meant a five-mile trek.

They wanted us to walk with them to the hostel but we managed to get out of that by saying we'd come later. We separated. Mo and I struggled up the hill.

"That was a waste of time," Mo said.

I grunted in agreement. It was only later that we realized how wrong we were.

It seemed to take hours to reach the cottage. The lower slopes of the hill were a maze of lanes. I lost my way more than once. We got more and more irritable with each other.

Luckily, I recognized Simon's cottage at once. It's near the top of the hill, just below where the woods begin. The old bit's built of crumbling sandstone and looks as though it's about to fall down. The new bits are painted white and the woodwork's black so the place has a piebald appearance.

"No sign of Davis," I said. "People park their cars on the edge of the lane by the house."

Mo groaned. "How are we going to get in if he's not there?"

"I know where they keep the key." I sounded more confident than I felt.

The cottage garden is even more like a jungle than ours at home. It's very private because of the high, ragged hedge which divides it from the road.

We scouted cautiously round the house and peered through all the windows. The place was empty. I'd been hoping against hope that Davis would be there. All the downstairs rooms looked just as they had when I saw them last.

"Well, where is he?" Mo said. "I'm getting tired of this."

I shrugged. I was too disappointed to speak.

"Come on," Mo said. "Where's that key?"

It was a relief to have something else to think about. I fought my way through the undergrowth until I hit a stone-flagged path. The path goes from the back door to the shed where Simon keeps his motorbike. Just by the path, covered by an iron square and shaded by a clump of nettles, was the stopcock for the water main.

I pulled up the cover and pushed my hand into the cool, damp hole beneath. The back door key was still looped round the handle of the tap.

"It's here, Mo!" I shouted.

"Shut up!" she hissed. "I can hear a car."

The driver changed down and was revving his engine for the last, steeper part of the hill. I told myself there were other houses up here, though none of them was close to Simon's cottage. The sound of the engine drew nearer and nearer. Mo grabbed my arm and pulled me up the path towards the shed.

We looked back as we went. A small blue dome seemed to be running along the top of the hedge. The hedge dipped, and we saw that the dome was fixed on to the roof of a white car.

The Ford Fiesta with the two policemen.

The shed was a confusing mixture of stone, wood and corrugated iron. But it was solid enough – and so was the big padlock on the door. We wouldn't be able to hide in there.

Beside the door was an old bath full of stagnant water. The end where the taps had been was half-hidden by a big bush. Honeysuckle or something, I don't know.

Mo jabbed her finger at the gap between the side of the shed and the bath. She burrowed into it and I followed, pushing my rucksack in front of me. The sunlight, tinged with green, filtered through the leaves. Mo curled herself up and I managed to get my legs under cover. One of her shoes was digging into my face.

It wasn't much of a hiding place. Anyone directly above would see us. As we waited I squeezed the back door key into the palm of my hand.

Two doors slammed. Someone unlatched the garden gate. There were footsteps on the path. The policemen were talking but I couldn't hear what they were saying.

Time passed painfully and slowly. When you're somewhere you don't know well, it's difficult to tell what the sounds mean and how far away they are. I heard steps, the rattle of door handles and the buzz of conversation.

Suddenly the voices were much nearer.

"What's up there, Jim?"

"Just a shed. I'll check it out."

Grass rustled. I smelled the tang of tobacco. A shadow cut across the green sunlight. Someone coughed, seemingly a few inches away. He gave the padlock a vigorous shake.

"No sign of chummy, Sarge," Jim said. "You want me to look round the back?"

"No. Come on. The next one's in Easton." The sergeant's voice was moving farther away. "Waste of time, if you ask me."

"Too right," whispered Jim, presumably to himself.

"He's skipped the country, you mark my words," the sergeant went on. "I mean, it's common sense. But you try telling that to the Drug Squad."

We stayed where we were until the coppers had driven off. I uncurled my hand and found that the key had stamped its outline on my palm. We wriggled backwards out of our hiding place.

Mo wiped her forehead with the back of her hand. "I thought this cottage was meant to be safe."

"They must be checking the addresses of Davis's friends," I said. "In a way, it's good news. They can't have caught him yet."

"They nearly got us instead," Mo pointed out. "What about something to drink? I'm not choosy. Water will do."

We walked down the path to the back door. The lock was stiff. When it turned, it shot back like a bullet. We pushed open the door and Mo dashed for the sink. I turned on the electricity mains. The switch is on the wall by the door.

Mo twisted the cold tap. Nothing happened.

"You are stupid sometimes," she said. "Why didn't you turn on the stopcock when you got the key?"

I never got round to answering that. Just as Mo finished speaking, there was a muffled bang from the other side of the house. It sounded as though someone had slammed the front door.

CHAPTER NINE

"Sam?" Mo said.

I was at the top of the garden, looking at the hole in the hedge. On the other side was a thick curtain of trees and bracken. For all we knew, an army could be concealed in the wood on the hill. There was certainly plenty of shelter for the person who'd been hiding in the cottage.

"Sam!"

I turned round reluctantly. I had this feeling that if I could have seen who it was, I'd have the key to the whole mystery. One thing was reassuring: he – or she – was more scared of us than we were of him. It made a nice change.

"It's no use," Mo said. "He had too much of a start. He could have gone down the hill or along one of the side paths."

"But who was it?"

"Don't ask me." Mo led the way back to the stopcock. "King Kong? Your guess is as good as mine. But he's not going to stop me having something to drink."

We drank mug after mug of water in the kitchen. Between us we must have put away nearly half a gallon. It should have been pleasurable but we were both listening too hard to be able to enjoy it. Mo dropped her mug in the sink when a bird started to twitter in the garden. In the country it seems so quiet that every little sound can be sinister. Especially when you're as jumpy as we were.

Mo refilled her mug for the fifth time and leant back against the table.

"So now what?" she said.

I looked at my watch. It was just after six. The bus had put us down in Gorbury at about twenty past four. The walk had taken longer than I'd thought. And now it looked like we'd done the whole journey for nothing.

"I'm staying," I said. "I'm going to wait for Davis."

She pulled her ear. "Look, Sam." She spoke patiently, as if she was about forty years older than me. "Davis isn't here, OK? There's nothing to show he has been here. You could wait for ever. Maybe the cops were right."

"You think he's left the country? Why should he do that?"

Mo hesitated before replying. "I know you like the bloke, but that doesn't mean he couldn't be a drug-pusher."

"But what about his brother – ?"

"The one he said died of an overdose?" Mo emphasized the word "said". "You don't know that's true. I mean, if I was a drug-pusher, I'd say things like that. Divert suspicion."

I shook my head. "I don't believe it."

"The police do."

I shrugged. My mother was gone and I still didn't know why or even if she'd gone of her own free will. My father had lied to me and betrayed me to Witcham and Trubshaw. Only Davis was left. I had to trust him, even if he wasn't here. But I couldn't put all that into words that Mo would understand.

She was staring at me over the rim of her mug. "So you're staying?"

"Of course I am. I've got nowhere else to go." I put my own mug very gently on the draining board, as though the stainless steel surface was as fragile as a cobweb. "But you go home if you want. You can have some money for a taxi. There's no need for you to stay."

Mo sighed. "You're as obstinate as a pig, you know that?" She put down her mug and walked across the kitchen to the door which led to the rest of the house. "Anyway, my parents think I'm not coming back tonight. If we're staying we'd better have a good look round in daylight."

She was doing me a favour, and we both knew it. Being Mo, she didn't make a song and dance about it.

We had already had a quick look and in fact there wasn't much more to see. The old part of the cottage had two rooms upstairs and two downstairs. The extension had the kitchen on the ground floor and the bathroom above. It looked like Simon used one of the bedrooms as a study. There was a desk by the window, with a computer and a typewriter on top, and one wall was lined with bookshelves.

I had the sleeping bag in my rucksack. Mo discovered another one in the cupboard under the stairs. So our sleeping arrangements were sorted out. Naturally she wanted to have the bedroom with the computer in it.

We found a lot of tinned food in a cupboard in the kitchen, enough to keep us going for days. I hoped it wouldn't come to that.

None of the rooms showed any sign of the intruder. Either he'd had a key, or there was some other way into the cottage that we didn't know about. Neither was a comfortable thought. I know it sounds ridiculous but we thought we'd better arm ourselves.

Mo got the poker because she saw it first. I found an old spanner. It felt heavy and cool in my hand. I tried to imagine what it would be like to hit someone with it. Would it make a noise? How much damage would it do? Would there be blood or just a sort of dent? What was the best place to aim for?

My imagination couldn't cope. I didn't even know if I'd have the courage to hit someone. I mean, think of it; bashing people on the head is the sort of thing you only see in comics or on TV.

Both of us were worried about security. We locked and bolted both outside doors. All the curtains were made of thin cotton, and Mo thought we should be careful about using lights when it got dark; a neighbour might notice them. We fixed up a sort of blackout in one of the downstairs rooms, reinforcing the curtains with layers of thick cardboard. It was so successful that Mo did the same in her bedroom.

The next few hours were like a dream in someone else's head. We did familiar things, like cook a meal and eat it, but in an unfamiliar way. For instance, we took turns to do everything so the other could stay outside the cottage to watch and listen.

This went on till just before nine. We were talking about the night and wondering if we should divide it up into two-hour watches.

61

Suddenly Mo said, "I've had enough of this. We need to sleep tonight."

I looked at her poker and she looked at my spanner. We started to laugh not because it was funny but because after a day like ours you have to laugh.

"We'll lock everything up, right?" Mo went on. "We'll put a barricade on the stairs. And if anyone comes we'll do a moonlight flit out of your window."

The moonlight flit wasn't such a stupid idea as it sounded. As the house was built on the slope of the hill, my bedroom window was only about five feet above the level of the back garden.

I caught her mood. "And then we'll hole up in the prehistoric fort and wait for the SAS to arrive."

Mo went upstairs, saying she was going to give the computer a road test before going to bed. I hadn't anything else to do so I thought I might as well watch television. There was an old black-and-white set, practically an antique, in the blacked-out room downstairs.

I switched it on, keeping the sound as low as possible. Earnest faces and city streets flickered on and off the screen. I remembered the TV crew coming to interview Witcham at the Imperial Spa. Of course it might not have been for the news; it could have been something for a documentary.

I found it hard to concentrate on the other stories. But then I heard the name of our city. Davis's face, enlarged, flattened and grey, appeared on the screen. I recognized the photo. It was an old one, taken years ago when his hair was much longer; it made him look like a retired hippy. (When I told Davis this, he said that was exactly what he was.)

I reached for the volume control. ". . . At a press conference this afternoon, Detective Superintendent Aintree said that police were anxious to question this man in connection with the arrest of a gang of heroin dealers earlier this week. He is Donald Davis, freelance journalist aged thirty-five. He is five feet eleven, has dark-brown hair and is lightly built. His car, a Deux Chevaux, was found abandoned this afternoon in a disused quarry south of the city. Davis may bc armed. The police have warned members of the public not to approach him. Instead they should get in touch immediately with their nearest police station or ring this number . . . "

They made him sound like a mad dog.

Then they started talking about unemployment figures. I turned off the sound. I felt glad that Mo hadn't been watching. For a moment I wondered whether I'd been wrong about Davis. Maybe he'd been fooling all of us for years. Seeing him on the news like that was a shock. You automatically think that the TV news is telling you the truth.

Suddenly I forgot about Davis. The television screen was showing a sign outside a huge building site.

WITCHAM BROTHERS LTD
INTERNATIONAL CONSTRUCTION

I lunged for the volume control.

". . . And the Council has announced that it will give its full backing to the Histon New Town Development. The project is the creation of Witcham Brothers, a locally-based firm, and was the subject of a public inquiry. The controversy centred on the fact that the Development site is close to Histon nuclear power station. The Council's decision was made public this morning, following months of speculation. A spokeswoman said that the project would be an "economic shot in the arm for the whole region". She added that the inquiry had shown that the safety record of Histon power station was second to none.

"In the afternoon, Mr Victor Witcham, chairman and managing director of Witcham Brothers, gave a press conference at the Imperial Spa Hotel in Easton. Mr Witcham's ocean-going yacht won the Kingdom Cup earlier this week."

The screen changed abruptly. I recognized the big room on the first floor of the hotel. This time it was full of people. Witcham was standing behind the desk and I could see Viney in side view. There was no sign of my father, Trubshaw or Iron-Face.

The camera didn't get too close to Witcham so he looked almost normal. He was leaning forward as he spoke, as though he was telling the audience a secret. His high voice was almost shrill with enthusiasm.

". . . I can promise at least twelve hundred new jobs in the next two years," he was saying. "The Development has already attracted substantial outside investment from the private sector, and the government is giving the project its support. As you know, we are very much alive to the environmental considerations. To be frank, I think our record shows that Witcham Brothers can be trusted to take them seriously. As for the health question, I'm glad to say we've received a categorical go-ahead from the relevant authorities. There is no risk of uncontrolled radiation leaks from the power station, either now or in the future . . ."

I'd heard about the Development before, without really taking much in. The local papers had been full of it. It was going to bring lots of money and work to the whole area. I dimly remembered Mum and Davis talking about it.

The presenter moved on to another story. I turned off the set and went upstairs. Mo was swearing at the computer. She sounds more and more Irish as she gets angrier.

I told her about the two things I'd seen on television. I must admit I played down the stuff about Davis – I just said the police were still looking for him and mentioned where they'd found his car.

"There you are," Mo said. "South of the city – nowhere near Easton. It can't be far from the airport – I bet he's gone abroad."

The old argument about Davis was just about to surface so I said I was going to bed. Mo wanted to stay up longer – she mumbled something about a computer file that was harder to get into than Fort Knox.

But first we went round the house together, re-checking the downstairs windows and doors. Mo wedged a couple of chairs between the banisters. We dragged a chest of drawers across the head of the stairs.

I didn't bother about undressing but I made sure I had my knife, the torch and the spanner on the bedside table. I crawled into the sleeping bag. There was a thin line of light underneath Mo's door. I heard the faint tapping of her fingers on the keyboard. A wind had blown up and the trees at the top of the hill were making a sound like the waves on Easton beach.

Tiredness weighed me down but I knew I wouldn't sleep. Too much had happened today. Memories were chasing through my mind. I knew I should think about what we would do tomorrow. We needed a plan. Mum and Davis had to be somewhere. People don't just vanish.

And then, much later, I was suddenly awake. I must have fallen asleep without realizing it. There was no longer a light under Mo's door.

It was much colder now. It felt like the early hours before dawn when you think nothing is ever going to wake up again. Something had woken me. Something near me in the darkness.

A bubble of panic seemed to race up my body. I knew it would explode into a scream.

"Sam?" a voice whispered. "Sam?"

CHAPTER TEN

Davis sat on the side of my bed. I can't describe the relief I was feeling.

"How did you get in?" I said. "We barricaded the stairs."

Davis gave a muffled laugh. "You forgot your bedroom window. It's easy enough to slip the catch with a knife."

"Where've you been? What's happening?"

He brushed aside my questions. "I can't stay long. Where's your mum?"

The relief evaporated. I sat up suddenly. "You mean you don't know where she is?"

"I thought she'd be here." Davis sounded disappointed. "What's she doing? And what's that friend of yours doing here?"

Then the truth hit me. I should have realized sooner. He didn't even know that Mum had gone.

"Come on, Sam. I'm in a hurry."

I swallowed. "She's disappeared."

"What?" For the first time he raised his voice above a whisper. He grabbed my shoulders and gave me a shake. "Tell me what happened."

I told him how I'd come home the day before yesterday to find her gone. Davis went very still. He made me dredge up all the details I could remember.

Apart from the occasional question, he hardly said a word till I'd brought him up to date. When I'd finished, the bed creaked as he leant forwards. We were still talking in whispers and of course it was dark. I could see him only as a shadow against the uncurtained window. Every now and then he looked at the illuminated dial of his watch.

"Shall I wake Mo?"

"No," he said. "I haven't got time. You sure you can trust

her?"

I nodded. Then I realized he couldn't see me so I had to say yes aloud. I wondered if I should mention that she didn't really trust Davis, not as I did. It was all getting horribly complicated.

Davis sighed. "God, it's a mess. And I didn't want to drag you into this."

"Into what?"

"I haven't got time to explain it all now. I'm meeting someone."

"Where've you been?" I asked. "And what about the heroin? Where does that come into it?"

"Oh that," he said dully, as if the fact that the police and rest of the world thought he was a dangerous drug-pusher was the least of his worries. "It was planted in my flat. I've got a friend in the CID; he tipped me off about the raid on Friday."

"But why didn't you stay and prove you were innocent?"

"I had something more important to do." Davis hesitated. "You see, I knew I must be touching a nerve if they went to the trouble of framing me. It can't have been an easy thing to do. And it was risky as well – the police aren't fools."

"Was Witcham behind that?"

"Who else? Oh, I can't prove it. You can bet he kept his hands clean. That sort always does."

I grabbed his arm. "And you think he kidnapped Mum?"

"Yeah." Davis sounded even more miserable than I was.

"So she's a sort of hostage?"

"You could say that." There was a rustle as Davis felt in his pockets. I guessed he was looking for his rolling tobacco. Then he changed his mind. "In fact it's worse than that. I think your mum's the only person who can stop the Development at Histon. That's why Witcham took her."

"But what's wrong with the Development?" I said. "I mean, all those jobs and things can't be bad."

"Everything's wrong with it," Davis said grimly. "Because they're siting it next to a nuclear power station."

"But it's safe, isn't it? The experts said – "

"I know what the experts said. But experts can make mistakes like any one else." Davis looked at his watch again. "Look, I've got to go. Can you manage here on your own? I'll try to come again tomorrow night."

I think I hid my disappointment. Somehow I'd hoped that once I'd found Davis everything would be all right again.

"Where are you staying?" I asked.

"I'm not going to tell you." He paused and added quickly, "Not because I don't trust you. But if the worst happened, Witcham might be able to make you talk."

I remembered Trubshaw and Iron-Face in the bedroom at the Imperial Spa. Maybe Davis was right.

He stood up. "You'd better not leave the cottage. If anyone comes, lock yourselves inside and keep your heads down."

"But, Davis – "

"I'm sorry, Sam. I've got to go."

I crawled out of my sleeping bag and went with him to the window. There was no sign of dawn in the sky. You could see a few lights on the other side of the estuary. The trees were still roaring and sighing to themselves.

Davis opened the window.

"Close it after me," he said. "I'll come back this way tomorrow. It's safer than coming round the front of the house."

He hoisted one leg over the sill.

"Davis," I whispered. "We're in a mess, aren't we? What are we going to do about Mum?"

"We're going to find her, that's what we're going to do." He sounded as though he was trying to convince himself rather than me.

I watched as he swung the other leg over so both legs were hanging outside the house. He turned back to me. "Take care now."

There was a thud as he hit the ground. The darkness swallowed him up immediately. I peered out of the window but I couldn't see or hear him. There was nothing to show he had been here except a bit of mud on the sill.

I closed the window and went back to bed. It was chilly and I was glad to get back to the warmth of the sleeping bag. As I slid my legs inside, I suddenly realized that there was one thing I hadn't mentioned to Davis: the person who'd been in the cottage when we arrived. It couldn't have been Davis himself because he would have told me. In any case, there was no reason for him to run away from me.

So who else knew how to get into the cottage?

The next thing I knew, it was broad daylight.

Mo was standing over my bed, shaking me. Once she saw I was awake, she went off to dismantle the barricade and make some coffee.

I didn't get up at once – I hate getting up at the best of times. The spanner, the torch and the knife caught my eye. Our precautions last night now seemed pointless, even childish. I lay back and thought about Davis's visit. Now we knew for certain that my mother had been kidnapped.

You know how you feel on the first morning of term? When the holidays are over and you can't get them back? That's how I felt, but a zillion times worse. It was like a weight pressing down on me.

Bed no longer seemed such an attractive place. I splashed some water on my face and went downstairs. Mo was in the kitchen, whistling while she waited for the kettle to boil. She found some cereal and made up some powdered milk.

Over breakfast, I told her what had happened in the night. She was really angry that I hadn't woken her.

"There wasn't time," I explained. "Davis was in a hurry."

"Charming," she said sarcastically. "I don't know what your mum sees in him."

"At least we know he's on the level now," I said.

"Huh." Mo sniffed, reserving judgment on that. She helped herself to more cereal and waved her spoon at me. "I suppose we know a bit more about what's happening. If he's telling the truth."

"Of course he is," I muttered.

69

She ignored me. "This New Town business. Witcham must've needed planning permission, right? Your mum works in the planning department."

"So does Viney," I said.

"Yeah. And for some reason Viney's backing Witcham. He can't be innocent because he knows about you and Trubshaw and Iron-Face."

"And about my mum."

Mo nodded. "I reckon your mum must have discovered something about the Development. And she was going to tell Davis, who was going to get it in the papers."

"Davis must've known something about it already," I pointed out. "He guessed it was Witcham who'd framed him."

"OK." Mo tugged her ear. "So your mum must have told him something earlier. When did they last see each other?"

"He was round at our place last Wednesday."

"That fits. Maybe she hadn't got any proof then, just suspicions. You sure they didn't meet on Thursday?"

I shook my head. "Davis was up in Birmingham all day. I think he spent the night there, too."

Mo chewed a mouthful of cereal. "Then Witcham must have realized what your mum was up to," she went on. "So he had her kidnapped. And he framed Davis so no one would believe him if he tried to make trouble."

"You've forgotten something," I said slowly. "What's my father doing in all this?"

"He's in it too," Mo said. "Like Viney. Witcham must have needed him to cover up your mum's kidnapping."

For a few minutes we ate in silence. I'd had all the pieces before but Mo had shaken them up and put them in a pattern. What terrified me was a possibility that neither she nor Davis had mentioned. If Witcham wanted to silence my mother, he might have done more than kidnap her.

It would have been much simpler for him to murder her instead.

"We need to track down your mum," Mo said at last. "And that means finding out more about Witcham. Where he lives, and stuff like that. Maybe we should go back to the city this morning."

I told her that Davis had said we should stay here, and that he'd come again tonight.

"Stay here?" she yelled. "Sit here and twiddle our thumbs? That's great, that is. What are we supposed to do?"

"You worried about your parents?"

Mo shook her head. Her face went sort of blank. "They're not really expecting me," she said, avoiding my eyes. "I said I might be away for a few days."

We argued about it for a while. I wanted to look for my mother, far more than she did. But Davis must know what he was doing and I didn't want to upset his plans by accident. There was also the point that we were safe here – at least for the time being. But anywhere else was a different matter. Witcham, Dad, Trubshaw and Iron-Face were after us. Maybe they'd set a watch on the roads and railways. It was also likely that my father had notified the police about me being missing.

Mo gave way in the end, though she didn't like it. She went back upstairs to tinker with the computer, leaving me to wash up. I spun that out for as long as possible – I even cleaned the sink and the draining board. I couldn't help feeling that my mother would have been proud of me.

It was still hot, but muggier than yesterday. Being cooped up in the house wasn't going to be much fun. I wandered through the downstairs rooms, staring through the windows and wondering about Witcham.

I couldn't understand what made him tick. I mean, he must be filthy rich already. You don't swan round in yachts and Bentleys if you're on the breadline. So why was he ready to break the law, just to make more money? Didn't he care that he was hurting people? Didn't he care about all the risks he was running?

Physically he looked so weird that at first I thought of him as a sort of bogeyman – an evil force that didn't need reasons for doing things. But somewhere behind the bogeyman there had to be a real person like you or me. And I had a suspicion that, if I could find that person, I'd also be able to find my mother.

Upstairs a chair scraped across the bare floorboards, making me jump.

"Sam," Mo yelled. "I've done it. Come and see."

I ran up the stairs. On the little landing at the top, there's a small window looking down to the lane at the front of the house. As I went past it, I glanced outside.

A Range Rover was coming slowly up the hill. There were three people in it. Seen through the windscreen they looked like ghosts. I recognized the two in front.

Trubshaw and Iron-Face.

CHAPTER ELEVEN

The screen was a jumble of light green words against a dark green background. It stood out vividly in the bedroom because Mo was working with the curtains closed.

I'd given a yell of warning as I was pounding up the stairs. She was already on her feet when I burst into the room.

"Iron-Face and Trubshaw," I gasped.

Mo pressed a button on the little box beside the VDU screen. A floppy disc slid out. She crammed it in its case and put it in the middle of a row of similar discs on one of the shelves.

"My window," I said. "Come on."

I led the way across the landing. There was no time to grab any of our things except my penknife and the rest of the housekeeping money. As I got to the window, I saw the backs of Trubshaw and Iron-Face as they went round the corner of the cottage. They were making for the front door.

Iron-Face was wearing jeans and an oil-stained red shirt. Trubshaw still looked like an old-fashioned advert for gents' suiting. He was even wearing a hat. My senses must have been working overtime, because every detail of the view from that window is still clear in my mind.

I yanked the handle on the window. The casement swung outwards. I clambered on to the sill. From downstairs there came a thud and the sound of breaking glass. Unlike the police, Trubshaw and Iron-Face weren't waiting politely on the doorstep.

I jumped. The ground rushed up towards me. As I landed, I rolled sideways like parachutists do. It was an accident, in fact, because I lost my balance, but it helped to absorb some of the impact.

I was already scrambling up when Mo plunged down

beside me. She managed to stay on her feet. It sounded like a rhinoceros was charging up the staircase in the cottage.

"The fort?" she said.

A hinge creaked.

It doesn't sound much but it was enough to stop us for an instant. The creak came from the gate which divided the front garden from the back. My first thought was that Trubshaw or Iron-Face must have stayed on guard outside the house. But I was wrong.

Victor Witcham laughed. It was a real laugh and that was why it sounded so sinister. He found us funny. He could do that because he thought we were unimportant. As far as he was concerned we were just a joke. To be exact, we were a joke that wouldn't be allowed to go too far.

"Dear me," he said mildly. "What enterprising children you are. Always jumping out of windows."

I had a split-second glimpse of him. He was only ten yards away but he wasn't making an effort to get us. He was leaning casually on the gate. He was smiling.

I think I shall always remember that smile. The perfect teeth stood out in contrast with the ruined face. The oddest thing was, his hair had turned blond overnight.

It was only a split-second glimpse because we turned and ran up the garden. We went through the gap in the hedge like a pair of human rockets. A branch slapped my face, just below the eye.

The wood stretched upwards. The trees were old and close together; the ground between them was an obstacle course of gnarled roots, bracken, brambles and green shadows.

Mo shot ahead, half-running, half-scrambling, through the undergrowth. Witcham was shouting something behind us. There were running footsteps on the cottage path.

I glanced back as I went. Suddenly Iron-Face crashed through the hedge. When he saw us he let out a howl like a wolf's. It was the sort of sound you associate with winter nightmares, not with a summer day.

I realized something at that moment. Iron-Face was mad.

Not just weird or strange or frightening – but mad, bad and out of control, like a dog with rabies.

The howl made us both go faster. The ground levelled out and then dipped sharply. I suppose we had run over the remains of the earth rampart protecting the prehistoric fort.

The middle of the fort had fewer trees. It was like a shallow oval bowl, covered with rough grass and dotted with rabbit droppings. We dashed across it to the opposite rampart. As we got there, Iron-Face and Trubshaw surged over the first rampart. A few seconds later they were joined by Witcham.

We ran down the other side of the hill. It was even steeper here, and much more overgrown. We did more sliding than actual running. Mo was still in front. I was remembering what the two French boys, André and Philippe, had said. I guessed that she had too. With Iron-Face breathing down our necks, we needed to find ourselves an ally.

Suddenly she stopped. I cannoned into her. There was another hedge here, with what looked like a new barbed wire fence on the far side. Towering over the fence, standing in the field, was a large white notice with freshly-painted red letters.

This land has been acquired for development by
WITCHAM BROTHERS LTD
Trespassers will be prosecuted
Beware of the Bull
KEEP OUT

We'd found the site for Histon New Town. We'd also found our ally.

The hedge was thickly-planted and over four feet high. Mo dived on top of it. For a few seconds she thrashed about on the top. Then she disappeared on the other side. I heard a yowl of pain and guessed she'd come into contact with the barbed wire fence.

I threw myself on to the hedge. It felt as though I was tossing and turning on a bed of thorns. Iron-Face was shouting something over and over again, like a wordless war cry.

I landed painfully between the fence and the hedge, avoiding the barbs but hitting my head against one of the wooden posts. Mo was already in the field beyond. She wasn't running. She was jumping up and down, waving her arms and yelling.

In the far corner of the field, the bull lifted his head.

I got through the fence, just as Iron-Face hit the hedge. He wasn't bothering with coming over; he was coming straight through. By now I was shouting as well. Mo and I began to trot away from the bull along the line of the hedge.

Iron-Face tangled with the fence. The hedge had ripped the buttons off his shirt. It flapped outside his trousers like a red cape. He gripped the top of one of the posts and vaulted over. Trubshaw's head and shoulders appeared on the other side of the hedge.

The bull snorted. He was a big brute, a real monster. Cows terrify me so you can imagine how I was feeling. The bull took a few faltering steps and stopped. He had another look at us, just to check his eyes weren't deceiving him. Then he began to move again. As he accelerated you could almost see his legs changing gear.

Iron-Face ran after us. We stopped trotting and went into a sprint. I heard a thudding rhythm growing louder behind me. I swear the ground was shaking.

"Pete!" Trubshaw yelled. "For God's sake! Behind you!"

I glanced back. Iron-Face was maybe fifty yards behind and he was no longer running. He'd swung round. The bull was almost on him.

Iron-Face looked tiny by comparison. I was suddenly sorry for him. It also occurred to me that he might even get killed, and we'd be responsible. For a second I didn't know whose side I was on, Iron-Face's or the bull's.

"Jump!" I heard myself shouting.

"Come on," Mo hissed. She'd managed to get over the fence again and was about to scale the hedge. I remembered our own danger and struggled over the barbed wire, collecting a few more cuts and bruises on the way. Mo's legs waved violently on top of the hedge. As soon as she was over, I followed her.

Iron-Face was nearly through the fence when the bull hit him. It looked like his shirt had snagged on the wire. One of the horns slammed into his shoulder. He gave a great screech, and the shirt gave way.

His body rose in an arc, turning as it went. He landed on his back on top of the hedge. Trubshaw, still yelling, hauled him down.

All this explains why I wasn't looking where I was going. I wriggled across the bed of thorns and rolled off the hedge. Without warning, an arm came round my neck and began to choke the life out of me.

We'd underrated Witcham's cleverness. Or maybe we'd just overrated his concern for Iron-Face. He hadn't stayed with Trubshaw. Instead he kept pace with us on the other side of the hedge, knowing that sooner or later the bull would force us over.

Mo was already in an armlock. It was so tight that she couldn't make a sound. Witcham's arms and shoulders were the strongest parts of his body. He pulled me down from the hedge, nearly breaking my neck. There we were, one on each side of him, like a pair of rugby forwards in a scrum.

Witcham shouted for Trubshaw. I stamped on his left foot, and Mo did the same on his right. He swore and tightened his grip still further. I could hardly breathe.

Trubshaw rushed up and grabbed me. He flung me face down on the ground, knelt on me and twisted my arm up towards my neck. I tried to shout but I had a mouthful of grass and earth.

I spat it out and managed to turn my head. Witcham had given Mo the same treatment as me. I could only see the back of her head. Witcham's eyes met mine.

He was flushed and breathing hard. There was a gap between his hair and his skin – a sort of hairline crack. He also looked strangely lop-sided because only one ear was visible – the other was covered with a mass of yellow hair. Above the exposed ear, all you could see was a purple band of scar tissue.

Then I knew why they called him Hairy. And why I'd seen a man with red-gold hair leaving Dad's flat. And how hair could change from white to blond in a single night. Witcham was bald. And he had more than one wig.

I think he realized what I'd seen. His face hardened but his eyes slid away from mine. He used his free hand to straighten the wig. At last I'd seen a weakness in him. He was vain.

"You damned fools," Witcham said. It took me a second to work out that he wasn't talking to us.

Trubshaw made an apologetic noise a few inches above my ear. "I'm afraid that Pete may be seriously injured, Mr Witcham."

"Serve the cretin right."

"I suspect a broken arm," Trubshaw continued smoothly, "and possibly a dislocated shoulder."

"He must have known that bull was there. He's visited the site before."

"Pete does tend to get . . . well, carried away." Trubshaw was pretending to be a stage vicar now, not a Hollywood butler. "He's so very keen, you see. Throws himself wholeheartedly into a job."

"Dear God," Witcham snarled, "you were chasing a pair of kids, that's all. Just a couple of kids, and you manage to muck it up. And there's that notice. Can't he read?"

"Reading isn't one of his stronger points, now you come to mention it." Trubshaw forced my arm a little higher. "It was providential that you were with us, sir," he added respectfully. "May I ask what you would like me to do with these two?"

Witcham thought about that for a moment. "Berkeley Terrace, I think. It'll be quiet down there on a Sunday."

"Yes, Mr Witcham. As we'll be passing the Infirmary, perhaps I might take Pete into casualty?"

"You can do it afterwards, Trubshaw. I'm not running a bloody ambulance service."

CHAPTER TWELVE

They weren't taking any chances on the journey.

First they dragged us back to the Range Rover where Trubshaw tied me and Mo together, her front to my back like a pair of spoons. It didn't take long because he used luggage ties. He dumped us in the well between the seats and covered us with a blanket that smelled of old dogs.

Witcham stayed with us while Trubshaw went back for Iron-Face. He was gone for quite a while.

None of us said anything. I just lay there in the darkness, with Mo's chin digging into the back of my neck, and listened to Witcham breathing. My muscles were aching, especially the ones on my shoulders and arms, because my hands were tied behind my back. I felt far more scared than I had when they were chasing us because I had time to think about it.

At last Trubshaw returned. I heard Iron-Face groaning as they got nearer. Trubshaw laid him out on the back seat and had a whispered conversation with Witcham. When we started moving, the groaning grew worse. It got so bad that I was glad of the blanket over me. I didn't want to see his face.

Witcham drove. I had no idea where Berkeley Terrace was but I guessed it might be somewhere in the city. After a while I noticed that the engine was cruising steadily and that we weren't turning corners. I reckoned we'd hit the motorway. That meant we were either going north towards Easton and beyond, or south to the city. Then I remembered Trubshaw mentioning the Infirmary. It had to be the city.

Iron-Face got so noisy that Witcham changed his mind about running an ambulance service. He stopped at the Infirmary and allowed Trubshaw to help Iron-Face into casualty. He kept the engine running while Trubshaw was away.

We drove on for a few minutes. The next time we stopped, I could feel Mo tensing herself behind me.

"All clear, Mr Witcham," Trubshaw said. "Shall I
unload?"

Witcham must have nodded. The blanket was twitched
aside. I blinked. Trubshaw stared down at me.

"I'd better help you, I suppose," Witcham said. "We
don't want another little accident."

They hauled us, still tied together, out of the Range
Rover. I knew at once we were somewhere down by the old
docks. There were hordes of seagulls and the smell of rotting seaweed that you usually find near harbours. We were
in the middle of the city but the only sign of other people was
the distant hum of traffic.

Witcham and Trubshaw dragged us along a path and up a
short flight of steps. As we went up, we passed another sign.
Like the one in the field, it had red lettering on a white
background.

THE BERKELEY TERRACE PROJECT
Another Inner-City
Renovation Scheme
by
WITCHAM BROTHERS LTD

Witcham ran out of breath before we reached the top, so we
all stopped for a few seconds. I had time to see that we were
in a cul-de-sac. On either side was a terrace of four houses.
You could tell that a long time ago they'd been very grand –
a bit like the house where Dad's flat is.

But times had changed. The terrace opposite had no roof,
and it looked as if the interiors of the houses had been gut-
ted by fire. On our side of the road, the ground floor windows and some of the doors had been replaced by breeze
blocks to keep out tramps and squatters. The front gardens
were full of rubbish.

Only one thing looked new: the door at the top of the

steps. It was painted black and fitted closely in its frame. Someone had stuck a poster for a rock concert on it.

Witcham pulled out a bunch of keys. There were two locks. The door swung back. Trubshaw pushed us into the hall beyond. I landed face downwards, sandwiched painfully between Mo and the bare floorboards. Witcham slammed the door behind him. There was an instant of total darkness before he switched on the lights.

Witcham opened another door on the left and turned on another light. Trubshaw pulled us into a huge, bare room. It had a carved wooden fireplace with a rusty grate, and it smelled of mould. Several of the floorboards were missing. Otherwise it was entirely empty except for a pile of yellowing newspapers in one corner.

"Separate them," Witcham said. "But keep them tied up."

Trubshaw obeyed. He took his time. I wondered if he wasn't used to doing this sort of thing. Maybe he usually left the sordid details to Iron-Face.

"Question time," Witcham said to no one in particular. "We can do it the hard way or we can do it the easy way."

Mo and I said nothing. In books and things, the hero's always ready with a smart remark when the bad guy starts making threats. But Mo and I weren't feeling heroic, more's the pity.

"Well now," Witcham continued. "Where's Davis?"

He stood there waiting for a few seconds, looking down on us with his head cocked to one side. He was directly below the unshaded bulb. Now I knew what to look for, I could see the thinnest of cracks between the wig and his discoloured skin.

"You must have seen him. Why else did you go to that cottage?"

Another silence stretched between us. Trubshaw lit a cigarette. The smell of tobacco seemed the freshest thing in that room.

"And I gather that someone's been keeping a motorbike up in the wood." Witcham raised the place where his eyebrows would have been if he'd had any. "Your friend Davis, I presume?"

The surprise showed on my face before I could conceal it. Simon kept an old Norton, a real beauty, in the shed. So that was how Davis had been getting around since he lost his car. Maybe he'd been sleeping up in the wood, near the bike.

I wondered how Witcham knew. Trubshaw had been a long time fetching Iron-Face this morning. Perhaps he'd been under orders to sniff around.

"Ah," Witcham said. "Struck a nerve, have we?"

He came a little closer and forced my head back with the toe of his shoe. I closed my eyes.

"As I mentioned before," he went on, "we can do this the hard way or the easy way. It's your choice."

Suddenly I opened my eyes. "What have you done with my mother?"

Witcham actually laughed. Then he gestured to Trubshaw.

"The hard way. You know what to do."

Trubshaw sucked deeply on his cigarette. "It's not really my department, Mr Witcham. Pete's our expert."

"Pete's not here, is he?" Witcham said slowly. "So it's your department now."

He stared at Trubshaw until the latter looked away. Trubshaw ground out his fag and left the room. A moment later he came back. He was carrying a pair of pliers.

Witcham licked his lips.

"The boy, sir?" Trubshaw said.

"No, no." Witcham sighed. "You've no imagination. No psychology. The girl." He turned to me, as if he wanted to share the joke. "Our Trubshaw's an ex-policeman, you know. Not a creative thinker. No policeman ever is."

Trubshaw hitched his trousers and knelt down beside Mo. Even at a time like this he didn't want to ruin his creases. He was still wearing his hat.

Mo swore at him. I mean, really swore.

Trubshaw looked over his shoulder at Witcham.

"The left hand first, I think." Witcham came a few steps closer and peered down at Mo. "Start with the little finger and work your way round to the thumb."

"Stop!"

I hardly recognized my own voice. I couldn't go on with this. I'd been hoping against hope that Witcham was bluffing. Everything was so unreal that it couldn't be happening.

Witcham looked round. "You said something?"

My nerve had finally broken, and he knew it. And I knew that he knew. And both of us knew he was enjoying it.

"What do you want to know?" I croaked.

"Don't, Sam," Mo said urgently. "Don't talk to them."

"It's no good." I couldn't face what they were going to do. It was as simple as that.

"At last," Witcham said. "A little ray of sense."

Trubshaw got up and dusted his knees.

"Don't rush away," Witcham said to him. "I may need you." He turned back to me. "Now look, young man. You've got yourself mixed up in something which you don't understand and which doesn't concern you. It isn't for children, it's an adults-only business. OK?"

I nodded.

"Good. Now we're getting somewhere. Have you seen Davis since we last met?"

I nodded again.

"Where?"

"At the cottage," I said.

"And when was this?"

"Last night."

"Why did you go there?"

"There was a postcard at home . . ."

"I see." He paused, biting his lower lip. "So you came to Easton because you were going to Gorbury? Not for any other reason?"

I shook my head. I saw what he was getting at. He wanted to find out if I knew what was going on between him, Viney and my dad. Maybe I imagined his expression of relief. It wasn't easy to read a face like his.

He bent down, so I had a close-up of the ravaged skin and the hairline crack. "What did Davis tell you?"

"Nothing," I said. "He was in a hurry and he wanted to know what had happened to me."

Witcham grunted. He glanced at Trubshaw, as though wondering whether to bring the pliers into the discussion. Then he changed his mind and prodded one of his stubby fingers into my ribs.

"Where was he going?"

"He didn't say. Honest."

Witcham prodded me again. "He must have said when he was coming back."

"He didn't."

"Trubshaw." Witcham waved towards Mo. "Carry on with the pliers."

Mo's face was almost as white as paper.

"All right," I said quickly. "He's coming back tonight but I don't know when."

Witcham took me through it all over again, asking the same questions and a few more that I couldn't answer. By this time I hardly knew what I was saying. But I did know that I was a coward and that I'd betrayed Davis. It was the price I had to pay to save Mo from the pliers.

When Witcham had finished with me, I felt as drained as a squeezed orange. He and Trubshaw talked quietly by the door. I heard Dad's name and Viney's, but not much else. It sounded like Trubshaw was protesting, and Witcham was overruling him.

Suddenly they were gone. We had no warning – the light went out; the door banged; a key turned in the lock. A few seconds later, I heard the front door close. I knew they'd be going back to Gorbury to wait for Davis.

The stuffy, windowless room seemed like a tomb. I realized I was on the edge of panic again. They could leave us here for ever. We'd grow weaker and weaker. Then we'd die, and the rats would gnaw our bones.

"Sam?" Mo said in the darkness. "Thanks."

I didn't reply. I'd been expecting her to be angry, even though I'd saved her from the pliers. There was a shuffling, scraping sound as she rolled nearer to me.

"I'm glad it wasn't you they were going to torture," she said.

"Why?" I was pretty sure it wasn't because she liked my hands the way they were.

"Because I'd've talked too. And I know more than you do."

"The disc?" I should have remembered about that before. In one way it was lucky I hadn't. I might have blurted it out to Witcham.

"There's a word processing program on that disc, right?" Her breath was warm on my cheek. "But there was also a file that shouldn't have been there. It isn't written in the same language as the others. It didn't even show up in the directory."

Then she started getting technical again. There were dot commands, ASCII codes, conversion programs and user groups. I got lost in the jargon after ten seconds. Mo was so interested in it that she seemed to have forgotten where we were.

"Hey," I interrupted. "What was actually in this file?"

Mo made a sound that was halfway between a laugh and a snort. "A lot of answers. Your mum knew everything. That's why they had to kidnap her."

CHAPTER THIRTEEN

It was very simple. Davis says most crimes are fuelled by fear or greed. This one was a mixture of both.

"It's a sort of letter," Mo said. "Your mum called it her insurance policy."

I frowned. "Insurance against what?"

"In case something happened to her before she met Davis. She'd only found out everything the evening before she disappeared. She hadn't had a chance to talk to him."

Mum had tried to phone Davis on Thursday night but he was in Birmingham on a story. The tape on his answering machine had run out. She didn't want to leave the house in case he phoned her. She was also afraid that Viney suspected something.

Mo had only had time to skim through the letter but that was enough to get the essentials. Her voice was husky in the darkness as she told me about it. She whispered even though there was no one to overhear.

It turned out that Mum had had her doubts about Viney for some time. He was strangely secretive about certain files. He came from a poor background and only had his salary from his job. But there never seemed to be any shortage of money. His kids were all at private schools. He took his family on safari holidays in Africa. They lived in an amazing house with a swimming pool and a sauna.

Once or twice she noticed that he was particularly interested in planning applications from Witcham Brothers. He tended to handle them himself, and generally approved them. The Council Planning Committee is meant to make the decisions; but in practice they usually took Viney's advice. After all, he was the Chief Planning Officer and had a list of qualifications a yard long.

Mum thought some of Witcham's applications should have been rejected. At first she'd assumed that she and Vincy just didn't see eye to eye. Later she began to wonder if there was more to it than that.

The crunch came with the Histon New Town Development. It was a huge scheme, and the profits were expected to run into millions. Witcham Brothers had invested heavily in it already. The Council and the Government wanted to back the Development because of the new jobs it would bring. But a lot of people were worried because the site was so close to the power station.

As nuclear power stations go, Histon is quite old – nearly thirty years. It has a Magnox reactor, apparently, which explained Trubshaw mentioning it when he and Iron-Face came to our house. The public inquiry generated a lot of controversy but in the end it came down in favour of the application. Viney, of course, had backed it to the hilt right from the start.

Davis knew about Mum's suspicions and had agreed to help her. She was expecting him to come round on Friday afternoon while I was at Mo's. They were going to plan their investigation. But of course Davis never came. By that time he was on the run.

"But on Thursday," Mo said hoarsely, "your mum found out about the report. A specialist one the Planning Department had done. Viney had changed it."

"But other people must have known about it," I said.

"Not this report. It was done by some consultants – a private firm. A sort of confidential survey of Histon's safety. It didn't say how they got their information. They sent it to Viney and he retyped the whole thing. All except one of their findings."

"How did Mum find out?"

"She accidentally overheard Viney and Witcham on the phone. Then she found the original report in Viney's private files."

Mo got technical again. It all boiled down to the concrete used to line the silos which held the radioactive waste. The concrete was specially reinforced with additives which were meant to prevent seepage. This particular type of concrete had only been used once or twice. One of the other places was in America. Hairline cracks had developed in their concrete because the additives reacted chemically with the waste. Over the years the radioactive stuff turned to sludge and leaked through the cracks and into the ground surrounding the silos.

The consultants believed that something very similar was happening at Histon, although the people who run the power station were keeping quiet about it because they didn't want the bad publicity.

"And guess who built that silo at Histon?" Mo said. "You got it. Witcham Brothers."

Viney had come back to the office while Mum was reading the report. She just had time to put it back but she wasn't a hundred per cent sure that he hadn't noticed something. Later that day Viney went out again. She looked for the report, meaning to photocopy it, and found it had vanished.

She had no proof to show to the Planning Committee or the police. But she knew that Davis would be able to help. He doesn't trust nuclear power stations. As a journalist he'd know how to ferret out the full story. She arranged to take the next day off work.

"Why didn't Mum tell *me*?" I said. "I could've helped. Why didn't she trust me?"

"Same old thing," Mo said. "We're just kids as far as they're concerned. Witcham, your mum, Davis – everyone. They think we're not old enough to understand."

I blew a raspberry into the darkness. We were the only people in the whole wide world who did understand. And we couldn't do a thing about it.

We talked for a while. It kept our minds off other things. Most of the pieces in the puzzle were beginning to fall into place. Witcham, of course, must have been bribing Viney for years. Trubshaw and Iron-Face were different. My bet was that Witcham had hired them to take care of any loose ends. I didn't know where my father came into this. To be honest I didn't want to think about it too hard. Not right now.

The worst thing was not knowing what had happened to Mum. The more I thought about it, the more I was afraid that Witcham had murdered her. He couldn't afford to let her go.

The physical pain was almost a welcome distraction. Both of us were getting more and more uncomfortable. I kept getting cramp in one of my arms. Mo was dying of thirst. Both of us – and this is something they never seem to worry about in stories – were bursting to go to the loo.

The conversation withered and died. After a while we just lay there on our sides, listening to the warm silence. Except it was never absolutely quiet. The old house creaked and sighed, as though it was settling deeper into the ground. And there were other noises – scratchings and patterings. Once there was a series of muffled thumps which seemed to come from the basement underneath us. Another time it was a rustle in the pile of old newspapers. Both of us gasped when we heard that, and the rustling stopped.

Mice? Rats? We didn't know. Whatever they were, the sounds were gradually coming closer. It wouldn't be long before the things that made the noises discovered us.

On top of everything else, I was worrying about Davis. He's a nice guy but he's not exactly in the Superman league. Think of Iron-Face and then imagine the complete opposite: that's Davis. He can't even see properly without his glasses. Witcham and Trubshaw would make mincemeat of him.

"Sam?" Mo whispered suddenly. "Did you hear that?"

I listened. The house was as silent as a tomb. Even the pattering and scratching seemed to have stopped. And then, just as I was on the verge of saying something to Mo, I heard a sound. It took me another second to realize what it was.

The stealthy scrape of a key in the lock of our door.

Forty-five minutes later we were sitting in a tearoom near

the cathedral.

There was a white cloth on the table. We had proper table napkins on our laps. We'd already made a dent in the plate of cakes between us.

It was the sort of place that I'd never have gone into by myself. But it was the first tearoom we'd come to after leaving Berkeley Terrace and both of us were starving. Mo said they could only chuck us out so in we went.

The room was L-shaped and crowded with tourists who'd come to see the cathedral. The waitress gave us a little table round the corner at the back. It was so dark and cramped that probably no one else would sit there. For the first few minutes we just ate and drank, trying to fill up the gap that had developed since breakfast.

Mo poured herself the third cup of tea. "The trouble with this business," she said, "is that it's one damn thing after another. As soon as we find out what Witcham's up to, another problem turns up."

I reached for the last chocolate éclair. She was right, of course. We had no idea who had rescued us or even why he'd done it. All we knew was that someone had come into the room where we lay. He had a torch which he shone in our eyes all the time. He undid the luggage ties and told us in a whisper that there was a window open in the room on the other side of the hall. He ordered us to go back to Mo's and stay there. Then he just went, leaving us alone with the darkness.

There was a very good reason why we didn't follow him to see who it was. When you've been tied up for hours, you can't get up. My hands and feet were numb. My body felt as though someone had been stretching it on a rack.

By the time we could move, the man was long since gone. In the room opposite, a sash window was a few inches open. The window was about eight feet above the ground outside. The bloke had dragged an old packing case underneath. Even so, he must have been tall to be able to haul himself up.

I wiped the cream from my mouth. It was lucky that

Witcham hadn't taken the money from my jeans.

"You know, that voice sounded a bit familiar," I said.

"You sure?" Mo said. "I mean, whispers are sort of anonymous."

I shrugged. "There was something . . . I think it was someone I know. Someone I've seen quite recently."

"Could it've been your dad?"

"No," I said flatly. That was one thing I was certain about. I only wished it had been Dad. It might have helped me to feel better about him.

Mo tugged her ear. "Well, that's not much help, is it? Got any other bright ideas?"

"We've got to do something." I ran my fingers through my hair. It felt filthy after being in that house. "D'you think if we went to the police they'd believe us?"

"Not a hope," Mo said. "We got no proof, have we? Even the marks are fading."

She held out her arm. When we left Berkeley Terrace, there had been red weals round our wrists and ankles. You could hardly see them now.

"Anyway," she went on, "the police would just hand us back to my parents and your dad. You know what that would mean."

We'd be back to square one. Worse than that, really, because my father wouldn't let me out of his sight.

"There's one chance left," Mo said. "Not a very big one but it's the only one we've got. If we can reach Davis before Witcham and Trubshaw do . . ."

Her voice trailed away. Witcham and Trubshaw had a good start. They had transport.

"Even if I could find Davis," I said unhappily, "how can he help me find Mum? He knows less than we do."

"Look, Sam," Mo snapped. "If we do nothing, we're finished. OK? But if we do something, at least we're in with a chance."

I nearly lost my temper with her. Then I realized she was right. I stood up, wondering how I was going to get back to Gorbury. I was also wondering how you paid the bill in a place like this – did they bring it to your table?

"I'm going back to Gorbury," I said. "You'd better stay. You've done all you can. Why don't you go home, like the man said?"

"Oh shut up, will you?" Mo pushed back her chair and waved at the waitress, who pointed at the till near the door. "I'm coming with you so you might as well stop arguing about it. And don't leave that woman a tip, she doesn't deserve it."

Mo swept through the tearoom to the till. There was a short queue. A woman was trying to come in from the street with a pushchair; she was shoving the door with her back. I held it open for her, hoping that God would maybe think that one good turn deserved another.

The woman came in backwards. She turned to thank me. For a second we stared at each other with our mouths open.

It was my stepmother Maxine.

"Stop!" the waitress shrieked as we ran out of the tearoom.
"Police!"

I swear my baby sister grinned at me as I skidded round
the pushchair and out of the door. Maxine wasn't able to
follow us because of Henrietta. But the waitress, waving
our unpaid bill, chased us through the hot, empty streets as
far as the sunken roundabout. We managed to lose her by
taking separate exits and then doubling back to the bus station.

Now we had another reason to be wary of the cops. We
checked the timetable and found we'd missed the last bus to
Gorbury. I remembered from yesterday that the Sunday
train service had been suspended because of engineering
work on the line.

There's a place where they organize minicabs near the
bus station. Luckily it was open. The only snag was that I
hadn't enough money to get us to Gorbury or even to Histon which is a few miles nearer the city. The bloke who ran
the place was quite nice about it but he wasn't going to lower
his rates for us. I asked him if there was a cheaper firm. He
shook his head.

I turned to go. Mo kicked me on the ankle. Her lower lip
was trembling and she'd made her eyes seem huge. She
advanced on the man behind the counter.

"Oh, please," she said with a slight lisp. "It's my step-
father. He'll murder me if I don't get back for tea."

The man backed away from her.

Mo sniffed artistically and carried on talking. The man
cracked after a couple of minutes. He admitted that one of
his drivers was going off-duty in twenty minutes. As the
driver lived in Histon, we might be able to make a private

arrangement with him.

So we sat in that shabby office for twenty-eight minutes, watching the clock and the door. The radio crackled away in the background. The bloke smoked four cigarettes and tried to avoid Mo's eye.

There's nothing worse than being forced to do nothing when there's a desperate need to do something. As the minutes crawled by, it seemed more and more likely that the police, the waitress or even Dad would come through the door before the man we were waiting for.

At last the driver arrived. Suddenly everything happened very fast. He agreed to take us at once. A few minutes later we were bombing up the motorway in his old Toyota. He was in a hurry to get home. Even so, he found time to ask Mo a lot of embarrassing questions about her family in Histon. She got out of that by saying we were just visitors, and that we were camping near the Youth Hostel.

He dropped us off in the driveway of the hostel. We waited until the sound of his engine had died away. It was very quiet after the city and the motorway. The hostel was stuck in the middle of nowhere between Histon village and the power station farther up the road.

For the first time since leaving the tearoom, Mo and I had the chance to talk about what we were going to do. Talking didn't really help. We knew from Philippe and André that it couldn't be far from the hostel to the top of Gorbury hill. What we'd do when we got there was anyone's guess.

The first part was easy. We walked down the road for about half a mile, until we reached the main entrance of the power station. On the other side of the road the fields sloped upwards, at first gently and then more sharply. It was the site for the Histon New Town Development. Right at the top was the fringe of trees which marked the earthwork. You couldn't see Simon's cottage from here because the hill was in the way.

Crossing the fields took longer than we'd thought it would. We had to go by a roundabout route, partly because of the new fences and partly because of the bull. By the time we wriggled over the last hedge, the sun had disappeared behind the hill. There was still a lot of light but the outlines of things were vague. The trees which masked the earthwork were crowded with shifting shadows.

Both of us were uncomfortably warm. It felt as though the fine weather might be about to break.

"What are we going to do?" Mo said as she brushed the leaves off her.

"We'll play it by ear," I said firmly. Saying it firmly made it sound as if it was a constructive plan, chosen from several options, not the only thing we could do. I wished we had a more impressive weapon than an imitation Swiss Army penknife.

Mo stared up the hill. "You do realize," she said softly, "your dad may be there?"

"Come on," I said. "Let's go. At least we've got surprise on our side."

I didn't want to talk about Dad. Maxine would know I was missing so the odds were she'd have tried to phone him. And Dad would let Witcham know. The plain truth was that my father cared more about keeping in with Witcham than he did about my safety.

We were as quiet as possible as we went over the hill. There was a nerve-wracking chance that Witcham and Trubshaw were waiting for Davis among the trees. They might ambush us instead.

It was growing darker now. There was just enough light to see where we were going. We hit a mud track which zigzagged down to join the end of the lane not far from Simon's cottage.

A five-bar gate separated the track from the lane. When we reached it, we stopped and stared at the cottage. Only the upstairs windows were visible. None of the lights was on.

I nudged Mo. "The Range Rover's not there."

"Well, it wouldn't be, would it?" she whispered. "Not if they wanted to set a trap for Davis. They'd leave it further down the hill."

Without going into the lane, we left the track and worked our way along the line of the hedge to the hole we'd used earlier in the day. From here we had a view of the back of the cottage. The first thing we saw was a light in the room downstairs where the telly was. The curtains were closed so we couldn't see inside.

"It can't be just Witcham and Trubshaw," I muttered. "Or they wouldn't risk that light."

"Not necessarily," Mo pointed out. "They might have put on the light to make Davis think we're still there."

"Or it might be just Davis – "

"Or it might be all three of them," Mo interrupted. "There's only one way to find out."

We climbed through the hole in the hedge. It was much larger than it had been, courtesy of Iron-Face.

It was lucky we knew the layout of the garden because it was nearly dark. The flagstones of the path made it easy to walk quietly. But we took our time, pausing to listen after each step. It was a bit like that game we used to play – Grandmother's Footsteps – where you have to creep up on someone from behind. Every now and then, the someone turns round and tries to catch you moving.

By now the window was no more than a few yards away. The curtains were quite thin. A shadow moved across them, distorted beyond recognition by the folds of the material. Mo, who was slightly ahead of me, turned round to whisper something.

I never found out what she was going to say. As she turned, there was a soft, metallic screech. We'd heard that noise before.

It was the gate between the front and back gardens. We couldn't see it from here because it was round the corner of the cottage. Mo beckoned to me and slipped noiselessly off the path. She crouched down behind a gigantic hydrangea. I followed. I dropped to my hands and knees and craned my head round the edge of the bush.

A man slipped round the corner. He was moving quietly and slowly, just as we had been. There wasn't enough light to see who it was, but I knew at once that it couldn't be Davis. This bloke was much taller and he walked in a different way, like a cat. (Davis walks as though he's got two left feet.)

He was working his way along the back of the house towards the lighted window. If he'd been a minute earlier, he would have run straight into us. He was passing the porch outside the back door when suddenly he stopped.

It was as if he'd doubled in width. It took me a few seconds to work out what was happening. Someone else must have been waiting in the angle between the porch and the back wall of the cottage. And now he was standing very close to the new arrival.

I strained to catch what they were saying but we were too far away. Then both of them went into the cottage by the back door.

The hydrangea blocked my view of the windows. I crawled away from its shelter. There was a chance that they'd turn on the light in the kitchen. If the curtains weren't closed I'd see who they were.

The window stayed dark. So did the window of the next room. But suddenly a slab of light crossed it as the door of the television room opened. I recognized both men with a jolt that felt like a kick in the stomach.

I wasn't that surprised to see Trubshaw. He'd just opened the door and was standing back politely to let the visitor go in first. The visitor passed from the darkness through the bar of light and vanished into the room beyond.

It was Davis's friend, Gary – the black law student. The bloke who told me that the police were after Davis.

'Well, who is it?' Mo hissed behind me.

'His name's Gary,' I whispered. 'He's got a room in the house where Davis lives. Trubshaw was waiting for him in the porch.'

'What's he doing here?'

'You tell me.'

It was weird but I wasn't scared any more. For a few seconds I was so angry I had no time to be afraid. Gary was meant to be a friend of Davis's. Yet there he was, on the best of terms with Trubshaw. It was another betrayal and it seemed so unfair. Davis didn't deserve this on top of everything else.

Before I knew what I was doing, I was back on the path and heading for the window. Mo tried to stop me but I shook off her hand. For all I knew, Witcham had a regiment of heavies around the cottage. Right now I didn't care. I had to find out if Davis was inside.

The rage didn't last. By the time I reached the window I was trembling all over and feeling sick. If Mo hadn't been there, I'd've rushed back to the hydrangea.

Mo was a few paces behind me. We crept up to the window, one on each side. It was slightly open. We heard Witcham's high-pitched voice quite clearly.

'Think of this as a citizen's arrest,' he was saying. 'Trubshaw will tell the police that you were trying to hitch a lift on to the motorway. Then, of course, he recognized you from the photograph on television.'

'You won't get away with it,' Davis said. 'What have you done with Sue Lydney? And where are the children?'

'Sue Lydney? I don't think I know the name.' Witcham chuckled. 'And which children had you in mind?' Then his voice hardened. 'Don't be naïve, Davis.'

'Better naïve than stupid,' Davis snapped. I'd never heard him use that tone of voice before. 'And you must be stupid if you think you can get away with this.'

'Not stupid,' Witcham said. 'Just rich. But I can't stay here chatting all night, much as I'd like to. Trubshaw and I have a few details to deal with.'

I pulled Mo away from the window. I knew we had to act fast, before they left the cottage. In an open fight we wouldn't stand a chance against the three of them. But I had an idea which could throw them off-balance while they were still inside. I told Mo, and she nodded.

Mo stayed by the window. I went down the path to the porch. The back door was unlocked. I slipped into the kitchen.

It was pitch black in there. Voices were still rumbling away in the television room. I ran my hands over the wall to the left of the door. They touched the covers over the electricity fuses first. Then I found the mains switch.

I pushed the switch. The click sounded as loud as a shot. But it was drowned immediately by an almighty crash of breaking glass.

CHAPTER FIFTEEN

But the gunshot was the loudest sound of all.

The glass from the window had just finished falling. There was maybe a second of dead silence. Then the gunshot. I don't know why people always say that shots "ring out". This one was like the crack of a whip but a thousand times louder. Perhaps the smallness of the cottage made it seem louder than it really was.

All hell broke loose in the television room. Someone was swearing; wood splintered; there were thuds and a cry of pain. I was moving forward, feeling my way through the darkness. I had some vague idea of trying to find the poker. Not that it would have been much use against a gun.

Suddenly the door opened and World War III surged out of the television room. The smell of cordite from the gunshot caught the back of my throat.

I forgot about the poker and concentrated on not getting hurt. I couldn't tell who any one was. I doubt if anyone else could either. I yelped with pain as someone crashed into me, shoving me back into the kitchen.

"Gary!" Davis shouted. "It's me you've got."

It sounded as though he was several yards away from me. I forgot about Davis as a punch landed on my shoulder. I ended up flattened against the wall where the mains switch was.

"Lights!" Davis yelled.

I groped automatically for the switch. Only the bulbs in the television room came on because all the other ones had been turned off before. But light spilled through the open doorway into the rest of the house.

The first thing I saw was Trubshaw. He was lying on his back by the cooker. His face was the colour of dirty putty.

He was breathing heavily through his mouth. I looked away.

The rest of them were almost as still as Trubshaw. Gary was on his knees. He was massaging his stomach. Davis was by the door to the television room. He'd lost his glasses, which meant he'd be half-blind. Mo, who must have climbed through the window she'd broken, was standing near him.

Witcham was the closest to me. His wig had been knocked off in the struggle. His head was a hairless dome, corrugated with scars. Like everyone else except Trubshaw, he was staring at me.

Before anyone else could move, he leapt forward and grabbed me in a bear hug. He swung me round as easily as if I'd been a doll. One arm slid upwards to my throat.

"One move," he said, "and I break the boy's neck."

He turned on the kitchen light.

Davis took a step forward, blinking in the harsh strip lighting. The grip tightened round my neck.

"I mean it," Witcham said. His breath ruffled my hair. "Where's the gun?"

"I don't know," Davis said.

Gary just shook his head. His eyes never left Witcham's face.

"It must be somewhere, damn you."

There was an edge to Witcham's voice. He sounded a bit like Mrs Jones does when she's about to get hysterical.

Davis turned his head in a wide circle. "I can't see it," he said slowly.

Gary grinned at Witcham. "Stalemate. Tell you what, if you let the boy go, we won't try to stop you escaping. Is it a deal?"

Davis nodded, agreeing with the idea. I realized now that I'd been wrong about Gary. He'd come here to help Davis, not to betray him. Trubshaw must have pulled a gun on him outside. That's why Gary cooperated.

I realized something else. If Witcham got hold of the gun, there was nothing to stop him killing all of us. Even if Davis and the others knew where it was, they wouldn't tell him. And it was no use one of them having the gun, because Witcham was using me as a human shield.

It all came down to the gun. Trubshaw must have dropped it in the struggle. If Witcham was thinking clearly, he'd know that he could make the others get it for him just by threatening to kill me.

"I think you look better without your wig," Mo said suddenly. Everyone else jumped. I think they'd forgotten she was there. "Ever thought of horror movies as a career?" she went on. "Or isn't the pay good enough?"

Davis and Gary told her to shut up. Witcham's breath was hissing through his mouth. His arm tightened so much that I found it hard to breathe. But I knew what she was up to. Mo had seen what Davis and Gary had missed: the importance of stopping Witcham from thinking clearly.

"Shut your mouth," he shouted at her. "Do you hear? Shut your mouth or I'll shut it for you."

I could feel he was shaking all over. I suppose he was used to everyone saying "Yes, sir, no, sir" to him. He'd got out of practice at dealing with insults.

"Stewed prunes," Mo said. "That's what it reminds me of."

"No deal," Witcham snarled at Davis. "I'm going, and I'm taking the boy with me. If you want to keep him alive you'll stay here."

The Range Rover was about a hundred yards down the lane, tucked in the driveway of an empty house.

Witcham drove back to the city like a maniac. On the motorway he pushed the speed up to 100 m.p.h. He stayed in the fast lane for most of the way, with his headlights on full beam. I was praying that the police would stop us. But God wasn't making any deals either.

He didn't talk to me. He just muttered to himself. Once or twice I caught the name Karen. Apart from that all I heard was the odd swearword. I started to think he'd gone off his head.

He must have realized that he'd lost. Too many people knew too much about what he'd been doing. Mo would give Davis the disc. Trubshaw, assuming he didn't die, would put the blame on Witcham when they handed him over to the police. Even if the Histon Development went ahead, Witcham and his firm wouldn't be doing it.

That was the good side. The bad side was that, if Witcham had lost, he was taking me down with him. And then there was my mother. I was beginning to think she must be dead.

This time he hadn't bothered to tie me up. We were going so fast along the motorway that only a fool would have tried to jump out.

Suddenly he looked at me. "How did you and the girl get away from Berkeley Terrace?"

"Someone untied us," I said. "I don't know who. We climbed out of a window."

Witcham grunted. The turn-off for the city was coming up. He cut across to it, barely slackening speed as we roared up the exit ramp. At the last moment, he jammed on the brakes.

"All this trouble," he said softly, "caused by a couple of kids."

While he was talking, I was trying to find the handle on my door. It wasn't easy in the darkness and in a strange car. Sooner or later he'd have to stop for traffic lights or something.

"You want to see your mother again?" he said abruptly.

I swallowed. My mouth was dry. "Of course I do."

"Then stop fiddling with the door. I'm taking you to her."

"Is . . . is she alive?"

He didn't answer.

We drove through the suburbs to the centre of the city. We passed the mainline railway station. As it was Sunday evening, there wasn't much traffic. We didn't stop once – even the traffic lights were on his side.

"Why?" I said. "What's it all for? You can't need the money."

"You'd be surprised," he said. "I've run that firm of mine

103

for over thirty years. When my brother sold me his share, we were just jobbing builders. Now we're one of the biggest contractors in the country. And that's my work. No one else's."

"Well, there you are. You're big already. You don't *need* the Histon job."

He laughed. "You wouldn't understand. You're too young."

"How d'you know till you've tried?"

I was curious about what made him tick but that wasn't the main reason I asked. I'd read somewhere that hostages stand a better chance of surviving if they talk to their captors. The better they get to know you, the harder it is for them to kill you.

Witcham shrugged. "All right. In business you can't stand still. Either you grow bigger or you grow smaller. If we don't get the Development, we're going to be in trouble. The creditors'll close in. One of our major creditors is a Continental firm that wants to take us over. If I do get the Development I can fight them off. If I don't I can't. It's as simple as that."

"But . . ."

"What?"

I took a deep breath. "Suppose you lost the firm. You'd still have money, wouldn't you? Surely they'd have to buy you out?"

"What's that got to do with it? Can't you understand? It's the firm that counts. *My* firm."

It still didn't make sense. He could always start another business with the money he got from the old one. The Infirmary loomed up on our left. In a few seconds we'd reach the sunken roundabout.

"But what's it all *for*?" I asked again.

Witcham took the second exit. We were heading towards the cathedral and the old part of the city.

"I had a daughter once," he said, so quietly that I could barely hear him. "Karen. After her mother left, she lived with me. Sometimes I'd take her to work with me. As far a

104

she was concerned, a building site was like a huge playground . . . "

He stopped talking. The Range Rover drifted along the street, as if Witcham had forgotten about the accelerator. The yellow glow from the street lamps gave me enough light to see where the door handle was. Without warning, Witcham grabbed my wrist and braked.

He brought his face a few inches from mine. "Then one day," he said, "there was a fire. No one's fault. We were demolishing an old factory and a drill hit a gas main. Whole place went up in flames. Karen was playing in one of the offices upstairs. I tried to save her. Oh God, I tried. She was seven years old. Do you think she . . .?"

His voice died away. His fingers were still digging into my arm. He was looking into my eyes as though he hoped to find an answer there for the question he hadn't asked.

"I'm sorry," I said. "Really I am."

It was a useless thing to say even though it was true. Witcham let go of my wrist and put his hand on the gear stick. I remember thinking that it must have been the fire that wrecked his face and left him bald. I was used to hating and fearing him. It made things complicated to have to feel sorry for him as well.

A drop of water landed on the windscreen with a splat that made me jump. Then another and another. A few seconds later the rain was pouring down. The windscreen turned into a waterfall.

I think Witcham was telling me that his daughter's death had made him the way he was, inside as well as outside. Maybe he meant that the firm was the only thing that kept him going since Karen died. Maybe he cared for his company like he used to care for her. Maybe getting his own way in business had become a sort of religion for him – a means of getting his own back on God or Life or whatever had brought together a gas main and the tip of a pneumatic drill.

I don't know. Perhaps he was right: I didn't really understand.

He switched on the windscreen wipers. We pulled away

from the kerb with a jerk. The Range Rover cruised along the green in front of the cathedral. I saw the darkened windows of the tearoom; it seemed like years since Mo and I were there. Witcham made a right turn after we'd passed the cathedral. I guessed we were heading for the old docks.

It didn't make sense. It looked like we were going back to Berkeley Terrace.

There were fewer streetlamps here, no pedestrians and hardly any cars. He knew exactly where he was going. We passed abandoned warehouses, modern office buildings and derelict houses.

Witcham turned into Berkeley Terrace, clipping the side of a car that was parked on the corner. He drew up outside the house and killed the lights. There were no streetlamps here, only a faint orange glow from the rest of the city. The rain drummed on the roof of the car. Thunder rumbled in the distance.

He opened his door and seized my arm. The interior light came on. I let him pull me across the driver's seat. He wasn't trusting me to get out by myself. Without letting go of me, he jumped down to the pavement.

The rain drenched him almost immediately. His light-grey jacket darkened. Water glistened on his head and ran like tears down his face.

"Come on," he said. "Jump."

Suddenly I heard running footsteps behind us.

"Witcham!" someone shouted. "Let him go."

It was my father.

CHAPTER SIXTEEN

Witcham pushed me back on the seat. With the other hand he lunged at the glove compartment.

"Dad!" I yelled. "Watch out!"

Witcham whirled round. His back was against the open door of the Range Rover. I tried to grab his right arm but I was too late. I caught a glimpse of my father. The rain had plastered back his hair. His jacket flapped behind him like a pair of wings.

The monkey wrench hit the side of his head. He fell sideways against the door and slithered slowly downwards. The back of his jacket caught on the window handle. He hung there with his head dangling forwards. Then he fell to the pavement.

I was scrambling out before he hit the ground.

Witcham seized me, first by the collar, then by an ear.

"You killed him," I tried to say. "Let me help him."

I was shaking so much that the words came out like a snarl. Witcham slapped me on the face.

"Hold your noise, will you? He'll live."

He pulled me away and up the steps. As he fumbled one-handed for the keys, I peered back. It was too dark to see much. Dad looked like a sodden heap of old clothes.

Witcham got the door open and flung me inside. He kicked the door shut and put on the lights. His eyes were even brighter than usual. He shoved the monkey wrench in his jacket pocket. There was a smear of blood on the bright metal.

"Get down those stairs," he said.

I did as he said because I knew he'd throw me down if I refused. The stairs led to the basement which was partly below the ground level outside. Some of the treads were missing so I had to take my time. The sweet smell of rotting wood rose up to meet me.

"Is my mother down here?"

The only answer I got was a prod in the back. The stairs made a left turn and reached a stone floor. There were two doors, one on either side of me. They looked new.

Keys jingled behind me. Witcham pushed past and unlocked one of the doors. He jerked his head, telling me to go first.

I don't know what I'd been expecting. Some sort of dungeon, I suppose. Mum chained to the wall and dressed in rags. Dirty straw on the floor. Perhaps the odd thumbscrew.

In a way the reality was worse. She was sitting on a bed with her feet up and a magazine on her lap. She was wearing jeans and had her hair tied back. Beside the bed was a chair, on which stood a lamp and a mug. There was even a frayed carpet on the floor. It all seemed so shockingly normal.

She looked up as the door opened. Her eyes widened when she saw who it was. I ran across the room and we hugged each other. She clutched me as if she never wanted to let go.

"You promised," she said over my shoulder. "You promised you wouldn't bring Sam into this."

"I didn't." Witcham closed the door. "He brought himself."

"Are you all right?" I said. "Have they hurt you?"

"I'm OK." Mum released me. She was still looking at Witcham. "What the hell's happening?"

He had locked the door on the inside. Ignoring us completely, he knelt down and rolled back a corner of the carpet. There were more flagstones underneath. One of them had a large iron ring sunk in the centre.

"I underestimated your son, Mrs Lydney." He slid the monkey wrench through the ring, using it as a lever so he could pull with both hands. The veins stood out on his face. His breath came in gasps. "Him and that friend of his . . . So did everyone else . . . As a result of which . . . I shall

108

have to – ah!"

The flagstone gave way. It was too heavy to lift out. Witcham swung it round on one corner and hoisted another corner on to the next flagstone. Then he let go. The slab landed with a thud that shook the house. I realized how incredibly strong he must be.

A current of cool air poured into the room. I heard the sound of running water. Witcham stood up, dusting his hands. He picked up the monkey wrench.

"It's a culverted stream," he said conversationally. "Runs down to the old docks. Much older than the house, of course. I imagine it was used as a sewer at one time."

I shivered, and not because of the cool air.

"A fine and private place," Mum said. It sounded like a quotation.

Witcham nodded. "One of my workmen found it when I bought this house. I thought at the time it might be useful in an emergency."

Mum swung her legs off the bed. "There's no point in killing us."

"Killing? Who said anything about killing?" Witcham slapped the palm of his left hand with the wrench. "No one's going to get killed unless they do something stupid. Come here, Sam."

My mother grabbed my arm.

Witcham sighed. "Something stupid, I said. Like disobeying my orders. I don't want to harm the boy, Mrs Lydney. But I need to take a hostage with me in case there's any trouble later on."

"Then take me instead."

I began to speak but Witcham ignored me.

"Sam's lighter and smaller than you," he told my mother. "And his age is another advantage. People are squeamish about risking a child's life." He took a few steps towards us. "Of course, if you won't cooperate, I shall have to use force."

That did it. I had a horrifying mental picture of the wrench coming down on Mum's head. I broke away from her and stood near Witcham. He looked at me and nodded. His lips were twisted in an odd way, almost as though he wanted to cry. I must have been mistaken.

"Sam – " my mother said.

"If he's sensible, he'll be quite all right." Witcham pushed me towards the hole in the floor. "You'll see him again. A week or two? A few months? Who knows?"

By now I was standing on the edge of the hole. The black, fast-flowing water was maybe four feet below the floor level. The sides of the culvert were out of sight. There was enough light from the room to see that something orange was bobbing on the water. It was an inflatable rubber dinghy.

Witcham's hobby was sailing, I remembered. This must be the start of an escape route he'd set up for emergencies. Maybe he had his yacht moored in the old docks. Part of them had been converted into a marina.

But in that case, why hadn't he taken me directly to the harbour in the Range Rover instead of stopping off at Berkeley Terrace?

Pushed by the current, the dinghy was moving from side to side. An oblong shape was lashed to one end. It was the size of a small suitcase and covered with shiny black plastic. Perhaps that was the answer to my question.

"Get in," Witcham said. "Just lower yourself over the edge."

I did as he said. My mother's face was drained of blood. Her eyes looked enormous.

The dinghy rocked as I landed in it. It swayed even more as Witcham came down beside me. For such an awkward-looking man, he was surprisingly agile. I suppose he was used to boats. His jacket snagged on the edge of the hole. The wrench fell from his pocket and splashed into the stream.

The culvert was at least five feet wide. The sides were made of rough stone which glistened with moisture.

"Sit down at that end," Witcham ordered. "You can make yourself useful by pushing us off the walls. Oh, and pass me the paddle."

He cast off. The current drove the boat down the culvert.

"Take care, Sam," my mother shouted. "If you hurt him, Witcham, I'll kill you."

The culvert curved. The dinghy swept round the bend and left the light behind. The darkness smothered us. The sound of running water was deafening. The bow of the dinghy jarred against a wall.

"Fend us off," Witcham snapped.

I obeyed him automatically. My mind was churning as I tried to calculate what was happening. Davis and Mo must have contacted the police by this time. Someone would check the Berkeley Terrace house. They'd know they were on the right track because of the Range Rover and Dad. They'd find Mum and she could tell them where we'd gone. The police would put two and two together and realize that Witcham was trying to escape by boat. They might be able to cut us off before we left the docks. There was still hope.

Witcham chuckled. It was a high, excited giggle. Even the memory of it gives me goose bumps.

"They say that smugglers used these culverts in the eighteenth century," he said. "There's a whole network of them. You'd need an army to block up all the exits."

I began to get an inkling of what was in his mind. I felt in the pocket of my jeans.

"People are so gullible," he went on. "Especially if you let them work an answer out for themselves. That way they have an added inducement to believe what you want them to believe. Because it makes them think they're clever."

I said nothing. I had the penknife out and was struggling to open the blade. My hands were clumsy with fear.

"You don't understand, of course," Witcham said with another of his giggles. "I left a trail for the police to follow. They'll reach Berkeley Terrace. Your mother will tell them how we left. So they'll hare off to the docks and waste half the night there. They'll have to search the estuary too."

The knife was open now. I jabbed the tip into the side of the boat. The heavy-duty rubber resisted it. I increased the

111

pressure and simultaneously twisted the knife.

Suddenly a torch came on. Witcham played the beam on the left-hand wall.

"We turn off soon," he said, "and go up another culvert. Eventually we'll reach a disused warehouse. It's owned by one of my companies. I keep a van there." He swung the torch towards me. He wanted to enjoy my reaction. "We'll have to paddle against the current, I'm afraid. We – "

He'd seen the red handle of the knife.

At that moment the blade slid through the rubber. There was a rush of escaping air. I used the knife like a saw to enlarge the hole.

Witcham dropped the paddle and threw himself at me. I rolled sideways over the side of the boat. I hit the water with a splash that sounded like an explosion in that confined space.

The water was much colder than I'd expected. I went right under and turned on my front. I tried to swim upstream while staying underwater.

I didn't have enough air in my lungs to stay beneath the surface for very long. I had to come up to breathe. My feet jarred on the bottom of the culvert.

The dinghy was less than a yard away from me. It was lopsided. Part of it was waterlogged already. Witcham was a dark shadow, clinging to the undamaged side of the boat. Splinters of light bounced off the water and the stones. The torch in his hand swooped towards me.

A crushing blow landed on my left shoulder. Simultaneously, the light went out. The impact must have broken the bulb. My mind was hazy with pain. I heard Witcham swearing. His high-pitched voice rose to a shriek which carried easily over the roar of the waters.

Gradually the screams began to fade.

I was standing chest-high in midstream, half-hypnotized by the unearthly sounds which came from the darkness. The water surged around me. I remember wondering if it was me yelling because of the pain in my shoulder.

The current was sweeping Witcham and the half-wrecked

dinghy downstream towards the docks. He couldn't steer without a paddle. He couldn't see without a torch.

Time passed. I was shivering. By now I could only hear the rustle of the water. That and my own ragged breathing. I couldn't move.

Then I realized that Witcham might come back for me.

Fear gave me strength. I turned round and felt for the wall. Half-swimming, half-walking, I struggled upstream through the darkness. All I knew was that I had to keep going. Sooner or later I'd come to the bend in the culvert.

It would have been so easy to stop and rest. I wanted to lie on my back and float on the water until I went to sleep.

But the water would take me back to Witcham.

CHAPTER SEVENTEEN

When I woke up the first thing I saw was Roland's face.

That's not quite true. Before I saw him I was vaguely aware of a bit of blue blanket and a row of tall beds.

Roland's face filled the screen of a colour TV. I shut my eyes and he vanished. Each of my muscles had its own ache. My left shoulder throbbed. I was very thirsty.

"They're regular guys," Roland was saying. "In fact you could say we're best mates."

I frowned and opened my eyes again. The TV was beside a big window at the end of the room. Three or four men in dressing gowns were watching it.

"Yeah, sure," Roland said. "I met Sam in Easton on Saturday. He told me everything. I mean, that's what mates are for."

Maybe I was dreaming. No, not a dream, because Roland was in it. That automatically made it a nightmare. I was too tired to think about it. At least I didn't have to look at him. I closed my eyes.

The next time I woke up, Mum and Davis were sitting by the bed.

They were holding hands. I've warned them before about being soppy in public. They don't seem to realize how embarrassing it is.

"Enough of that," I croaked.

I tried to sit up. My shoulder exploded with pain. I discovered that my left arm was strapped to my body.

Mum bent down and kissed me. "You're in the Infirmary," she said. "You got yourself a broken collarbone."

Davis grinned at me. He was wearing his old glasses, the ones that are held together with Sellotape. I noticed that he hadn't got around to shaving for some time.

114

I felt relieved to see them without knowing why. A second later I remembered everything. Everything up to the moment when I struggled round the bend in the culvert and saw the light pouring down from the basement.

"Where's Dad?" I said.

"Your father's OK, just a bit concussed," Mum said. "In fact he's in the next ward."

"And what about Witcham?"

Mum glanced quickly at Davis. "He was swept down to the old docks."

"So they got him?"

She shook her head. "They . . . they found his body."

I frowned. "You mean he drowned?"

"Apparently he couldn't swim." Mum leant forward. "Try not to think about it. Maybe it was the best thing that could've happened. It's all over now. That's the main thing."

"But it doesn't make sense," I said. "The stream wasn't that deep. I could stand up in it – so why couldn't he?"

"We'll never know," Davis said, "not for sure. I suppose he might have hit his head."

I looked at Mum. "What do you think?"

She shrugged. "I wonder if he just gave up. He didn't have much to live for. Just a long prison sentence."

There was a moment's silence. I was thinking about what Witcham said in the Range Rover.

"Did you know about his daughter?" I asked. "Karen?"

Mum nodded. "He told me about that. It explains quite a lot."

Davis looked over his shoulder. A nurse at the other end of the ward was having an argument with someone. Her voice was getting louder and louder. She sounded like a real old dragon.

"I don't care who you are. You'll just have to wait until visiting time. Come back! Come back!"

Mo was running down the ward. I started to laugh.

I hate stories that leave you guessing at the end. You know

the sort that don't tie up all the loose ends. This is as good a place as any to make a few knots.

They let me out of hospital late that afternoon. Mum and Davis took me home in a taxi. The house looked like a typhoon had been through it. Trubshaw and Iron-Face had come back after they failed to catch us on Saturday morning.

The press wanted to see us. Mo and I were heroes, not that it did us much good. Mo's parents practically put her under house arrest and Mum wouldn't let me talk to journalists, except Davis who doesn't count. It really made me mad.

The police interviewed us several times over the next few days. At the same time they were able to answer a lot of our questions.

Trubshaw and Iron-Face were both in jail, waiting for their trial to come up. Neither of them was badly injured. Trubshaw really had been a policeman – he'd been sacked for reselling confiscated drugs. Then he'd teamed up with Iron-Face, whom he'd met in prison. They called themselves security consultants. Trubshaw still had friends in the police. He persuaded one of them to give him a photocopy of Davis's address book. That was how they found out about Simon's cottage. Witcham thought it was a likely place for Davis to go because it's so near Histon.

Mum was kidnapped by Iron-Face and Witcham. Viney had realized that she knew about the fake report. They were worried that she might have told Davis, which was why they'd decided to deal with him too. Witcham suspected all along that Mum had left a message for him. When Mo and I turned up on Saturday morning, he guessed we might have found it.

It was Trubshaw who framed Davis as a drug-pusher. He broke into Davis's flat, planted the heroin and tipped off the police anonymously. Davis got early warning about the bust from his CID contact. He realized it must have something to do with the Histon business. He managed to tell Gary what was happening. Gary got rid of the Deux Chevaux in an attempt to throw everyone off the scent.

You remember the mysterious intruder at Simon's cottage? That was Gary – he'd arranged to meet Davis there. And Gary, of course, was the man who rescued Mo and me from Berkeley Terrace on Sunday afternoon. He followed Witcham and Trubshaw there on Saturday night. He didn't know we were inside – only that Witcham was using the place as a base. Finding us was a real shock to him.

Gary was in too much of a hurry to search the rest of the house. He'd missed his rendezvous with Davis the previous night so he didn't even know that Mum was missing. It turned out that she was making the muffled thumps we heard while we were tied up.

At first I couldn't understand why Gary didn't tell us who he was. He tried to explain: it was vital that Witcham shouldn't discover he was working with Davis; he was Davis's one link with the outside world. He had no idea we already knew so much. How could he? Only Davis could have told him.

I can see that. What sticks in my throat is that Gary didn't identify himself to us because he was afraid we'd tell someone – Dad, or even Witcham if he managed to recapture us. In other words it was the same old story: like everyone else, Gary thought we were just kids and couldn't be trusted to keep our mouths shut.

To give him his due, he came round and apologized for underrating us. Mo told him she hoped he'd have more sense next time. Gary said he hoped there wouldn't be a next time. So do I.

As my mother suspected, Viney had been taking bribes from Witcham for years. It had started quite innocently when Viney desperately wanted money to pay for an operation his wife needed. Witcham offered him a loan. Viney couldn't repay him in cash so Witcham suggested another way. Once he'd started, Viney couldn't stop because Witcham threatened to expose him. They arrested Viney on Monday afternoon at the airport.

Police frogmen found Witcham's suitcase in the culvert.

It contained a false passport, a lot of foreign currency and negotiable securities. There was also a photograph album. All the pictures were of Karen.

It looks like the Histon Development will be cancelled. Witcham's firm has folded. They're going to have an inquiry about the hairline cracks in the power station's silos. After all the publicity no one would want to live or work next door.

No, I haven't forgotten. There's another loose end that needs tying up. My father.

I went to see him at the flat, a couple of days after I came out of hospital.

Maxine let me in. For once she wasn't wearing make-up. Her eyes were red-rimmed. She was carrying Henrietta who belched when she saw me.

Dad was in bed. The curtains were closed. He had a huge bandage on his head that made him look like an unemployed rajah. His face was pale, and he seemed to have lost weight.

Maxine left us alone. I think we were both grateful for that. There was a moment's silence, during which I wished I hadn't come.

"I've been lying here," he said at last, "wondering what to say to you."

I shrugged. "I think I know most of it."

Mum had told me that Dad's firm handled Witcham's advertising, and that Dad was the executive in charge of the account. I also knew that Dad had been sacked.

"I'm sorry," he said. "Really."

"That's OK."

It wasn't OK but I had to say something.

"I've been so damned stupid," he went on. "It started in such a small way. There always seemed to be something I needed to buy. And then it got out of control."

His story was a bit like Viney's except Dad hadn't been so deeply involved until very recently. Witcham had given him loans and presents in return for favours. Some of the

118

favours had been illegal or at least shady. There was something about allowing Witcham to use him as a front in financial deals to evade tax.

Then last week Witcham turned up at Dad's flat while Maxine and Henrietta were out. He asked Dad to look after me and not make a fuss about Mum's disappearance. Dad lost his temper and refused. Witcham just smiled and went away. A few minutes later he came back with Iron-Face.

Witcham barged into Henrietta's bedroom. Iron-Face had a bottle of vitriol in his pocket. You know what vitriol is? Concentrated sulphuric acid. If you put a body in a bath of vitriol, it sucks all the water out of the tissues. The body turns to sludge. Everything dissolves, even the bones.

Witcham kept smiling while Iron-Face sprinkled a few drops of acid on the mattress of the cot. They burned through the sheet, through the plastic and the foam rubber, and scarred the wood underneath. And all the while Witcham was talking.

He wasn't going to hurt Mum, he said, just keep her out of circulation until the Development was safely under way. Dad had a choice: if he agreed, he would get a lot of money (including my school fees); if he refused, Witcham was going to get my father sacked and set Iron-Face on to Maxine and Henrietta.

"Think of their faces," Witcham had said. "Their eyes, for example. I'm told it has a charring effect – rather like a burn. It wouldn't take much. Just a few drops."

"The big stick," Dad went on, "and the big carrot. That's how Witcham worked." He put his head in his hands. "I just kept thinking about what vitriol would do to them. I dreamed about it too."

"Did you believe him?" I asked.

"Believe what?"

"That he wouldn't hurt Mum."

"I . . . I wanted to believe him." My father stared at his hands. "So I did. I'll never forgive myself for that."

Neither of us said anything for a few minutes. I think Dad wanted to ask if Mum and I could forgive him. It was a question I didn't want to answer.

Witcham would have never let my mother go: she knew too much. He had to kill her. My guess is that he only kept her alive in case he needed a lever to use against Davis. Once Davis was caught, Witcham would have murdered her.

Funnily enough, Mum doesn't agree. She thinks that Witcham didn't have the heart to kill her after he'd told her about Karen.

Dad didn't say so but I reckon Maxine's got a lot to answer for. I think she bullies him. He could never earn quite enough for her. He didn't tell her about the vitriol – after Witcham and Iron-Face left, he rushed out and bought a new sheet and mattress for the cot. It seems a funny sort of marriage to me.

My father cleared his throat. "Maxine told me she'd seen you on Sunday," he said. "And about you running away. That's when I decided I couldn't go on with this, that I'd break with Witcham once and for all. I told Maxine about the vitriol. Then I drove her and Henrietta over to her mother's. After that I looked for Witcham. I couldn't find him but I knew he'd come back to Berkeley Terrace. So I waited outside in the car."

"Did you know that Mum was in the cellar?"

He shook his head. "Just that Witcham was spending a lot of time there. And then you arrived." He looked away from me. "I even managed to mess that up."

"I don't know," I said. "At least you tried."

I wanted to say that I was glad that he'd seen sense at last, and glad that he'd tried to help me. If he hadn't I wouldn't have come to see him. Ever. In a strange way knowing why made it easier to cope with. I don't know if I'd think straight if someone was mucking around with vitriol. It sort of reminded me of Mo and the pliers. It was too complicated to explain. I sat down on the end of the bed.

"Did your mother tell you they're going to prosecute me?" he asked.

I nodded.

"And we'll have to sell this flat. Can't say I'm sorry. I never really liked it."

"Nor me."

We smiled at each other like a pair of conspirators.

Dad's smile slipped. "I might have to go to prison."

"I know that too." I played with the edge of the duvet. "But it might not happen. And if it does, it won't be for long, will it? Maybe they'll let me come and see you."

I tried to speak cheerfully. It was hard to know how to handle this. Over the last few days our positions seemed to have been reversed. It was almost as if he'd grown younger and I'd grown older. He was the one who needed looking after.

"I'd like that," my father said. "If you're sure you wouldn't mind."

"I'm going to buy a new car," Davis said.

"You can't afford it," my mother pointed out.

It was the Saturday after the weekend which had nearly ruined our lives. We were sitting in our jungle garden. Davis and I were playing chess. Mo was there too. She said she'd come to cheer me up.

"I will be able to," Davis said. "Once I've signed the contract."

You can't trust anyone these days. He's going to write about the Witcham affair for one of the Sunday papers. He's finally sold out to the establishment. When I told him this he said he'd only rented himself out on a temporary basis.

"If you had any sense," Mo said, "you'd use the money to buy a word processor."

Davis moved his bishop and passed the travelling chess set to me. "No need. I can use Sue's."

He and my mother have at last decided that they might as well live together. I don't know why he didn't move in years ago. But they're not getting married. Mum says that once was enough.

I bent over the chessboard. Davis was going to checkmate

121

me in three moves, and there was nothing I could do about it. I closed the set with a snap and chucked it on the grass.

To be honest, they were all irritating me. Mum and Davis had each other. Davis was going to earn some money for once. My mother was getting promoted because of Viney's departure. Mo could do whatever she wanted with the rest of the summer holidays. She was going swimming almost every day.

And here I was, stuck at home with a broken collarbone. Our doctor hadn't helped: he told Mum that I shouldn't exert myself too much over the next week or two. So what was I supposed to do?

Mo went into the kitchen to fetch us another Coke.

"I'm bored," I said to no one in particular.

"Tell you what," Davis said. "You could do some work for me. It'd be a help to have your side of the story – I could use it in the articles. I'd pay you something, of course."

I though about it for a moment. Maybe Mo would teach me how to use a word processor. All I had to describe was one weekend. I'd start with the Friday afternoon when I arrived home to an empty house.

"All right," I said. "I will."

And so I have.

The Pit

ANN CHEETHAM

The summer has hardly begun when Oliver Wright is plunged into a terrifying darkness. Gripped by fear when workman Ted Hoskins is reduced to a quivering child at a demolition site, Oliver believes something of immense power has been disturbed. But what?

Caught between two worlds – the confused present and the tragic past – Oliver is forced to let events take over.

£2.50 ☐

Nightmare Park

LINDA HOY

A highly original and atmospheric thriller set around a huge modern theme park, a theme park where teenagers suddenly start to disappear . . .

£2.50 ☐

ARMADA

Run With the Hare

LINDA NEWBERY

A sensitive and authentic novel exploring the workings of an animal rights group, through the eyes of Elaine, a sixth-form pupil. Elaine becomes involved with the group through her more forceful friend Kate, and soon becomes involved with Mark, an Adult Education student and one of the more sophisticated members of the group. Elaine finds herself painting slogans and sabotaging a fox hunt. Then she and her friends uncover a dog fighting ring – and things turn very nasty.

£2.50 ☐

Hairline Cracks

JOHN ROBERT TAYLOR

A gritty, tense and fast-paced story of kidnapping, fraud and cover ups. Sam Lydney's mother knows too much. She's realized that a public inquiry into the safety of a nuclear power station has been rigged. Now she's disappeared and Sam's sure she has been kidnapped, he can trust no one except his resourceful friend Mo, and together they are determined to uncover the crooks' operation and, more importantly, find Sam's mother.

£2.50 ☐

ARMADA

Armada
Gift Classics

An attractive collection of beautifully illustrated stories, including some of the finest and most enjoyable children's stories ever written.

Some of the older, longer titles have been skilfully edited and abridged.

Little Women	Louisa M. Alcott	£2.25	☐
Peter Pan	J. M. Barrie	£2.25	☐
The Wizard of Oz	L. Frank Baum	£1.95	☐
Lorna Doone	R. D. Blackmore	£1.95	☐
What Katy Did	Susan M. Coolidge	£2.25	☐
What Katy Did at School	Susan M. Coolidge	£1.95	☐
What Katy Did Next	Susan M. Coolidge	£1.95	☐
The Wind in the Willows	Kenneth Grahame	£2.25	☐
The Secret Garden	Frances Hodgson Burnett	£2.25	☐
The Phantom of the Opera	Gaston Leroux	£1.95	☐
The Railway Children	E. Nesbit	£1.95	☐
The Scarlet Pimpernel	Baroness Orczy	£1.95	☐
Black Beauty	Anna Sewell	£1.95	☐
Kidnapped	R. L. Stevenson	£1.95	☐
Treasure Island	R. L. Stevenson	£1.95	☐
Dracula	Bram Stoker	£1.95	☐
Gulliver's Travels	Jonathan Swift	£1.95	☐
The Adventures of Tom Sawyer	Mark Twain	£1.95	☐
Around the World in 80 Days	Jules Verne	£2.25	☐

ARMADA

All these books are available at your local bookshop or newsagent, or can be ordered from the publisher. To order direct from the publishers just tick the title you want and fill in the form below:

Name _____

Address _____

_____

Send to: HarperCollins Children's Cash Sales
PO Box 11
Falmouth
Cornwall
TR10 9EN

Please enclose a cheque or postal order or debit my Visa/Access –

        Credit card no:
        Expiry date:
        Signature:

– to the value of the cover price plus:
UK: 60p for the first book, 25p for the second book, plus 15p per copy for each additional book ordered to a maximum charge of £1.90.

BFPO: 60p for the first book, 25p for the second book plus 15p per copy for the next 7 books, thereafter 9p per book.

Overseas and Eire: £1.25 for the first book, 75p for the second book. Thereafter 28p per book.